MW00778242

Neil

CHRIS
KENISTON

Indie House Publishing

Print Edition

MORE BOOKS

By Chris Keniston

Hart Land

Heather
Lily
Violet
Iris
Hyacinth
Rose
Calytrix
Zinnia
Poppy
Picture Perfect

Farraday Country

Adam
Brooks
Connor
Declan
Ethan
Finn
Grace
Hannah
Ian
Jamison
Keeping Eileen
Loving Chloe
Morgan
Neil

Honeymoon Series

Honeymoon for One
Honeymoon for Three
Honeymoon for Four

Honeymoon for Five

Aloha Romance Series:

Aloha Texas
Almost Paradise
Mai Tai Marriage
Dive Into You
Look of Love
Love by Design
Love Walks In
Shell Game
Flirting with Paradise

Surf's Up Flirts:

(Aloha Series Companions)

Shall We Dance
Love on Tap
Head Over Heels
Perfect Match
Just One Kiss
It Had to Be You
Cat's Meow

ACKNOWLEDGMENT

It's always fun for me to return to Farraday Country. The Farradays are like old friends and I love visiting and seeing the family grow, but it wouldn't be possible without a lot of help.

Once again my books come together with the love and support of my friends. Both writers and readers. I have to thank Laura Scott for making sure I didn't botch the healthcare scenes. Any and all mistakes are all mine. Susan Warner once again came to my rescue when the blank page was staring back at me for hours on end. Olivia Sands for having a brilliant veterinarian daughter and being willing to share her knowledge with me. Kathy Ivan for her creative input in avoiding the expected. My hubby for letting me write all night and sleep in all morning.

I hope you all enjoy this story as much as we have.

Thanks for sticking with me as all the brothers and cousins fall in love!

CHAPTER ONE

This was a really dumb idea. Nora Brown stared at the screen in front of her, one finger poised over the enter key that would send her response through cyberspace.

"You okay?" Brooks Farraday dropped a patient folder into the to-be-filed box. "You look a little green around the gills."

"Really? I feel fine." She couldn't put on a straight face if she tried. The fact that she teetered somewhere between terrified and jubilant was probably a contributing factor to the urge to throw up.

Brooks' brows crinkled together before he shook it off and proceeded to exam room two where the Montgomery triplets were in for their annual checkup.

Once again holding her finger over the keyboard, she looked at the photo on the screen. Nice face. Nothing special. Nothing scary. Just another nice face. Ted, the first candidate to catch her attention, had had a nice face. For almost a month the messages they'd shared had been nothing to write home about but she'd looked forward to each and every communication. The little internet flirtation had been the closest thing she'd done to steady dating since college.

Though she'd never thought it possible, with all of her friends happily married off and now having babies, and the Saturday afternoon Ladies Social Club card game the most exciting part of her week, she felt as if her best years were behind her. Like she should take up knitting and cat collecting. And at her age that was the dumbest thing she'd ever heard of. So, without any decent prospects in Tuckers

Bluff, she'd embraced the internet and gone hunting for a date not too far from town, but not too close. No point in looking in Tuckers Bluff and no point in letting the grapevine learn she was looking for a man online. That's how she'd found Ted. She wasn't sure quite what went wrong but the communication slowed and then stopped all together. That led to the next nice face, Brandon.

At least his emails had been more entertaining. An efficiency consultant, he traveled quite a bit which didn't thrill her, but he had a fun sense of humor and she'd liked how easily he could make her laugh. In the end, that potential relationship fizzled as well. She was beginning to wonder if there was something really wrong with her. So many dating apps and so little success, but what other choice did she have? The risk of being ghosted once again was worth it. *Maybe.*

So here she sat looking at another nice face on her screen. A used laser equipment salesman who was ready for someone more permanent in his life. Unlike the others, this time he wanted to meet her face to face. Here. In Tuckers Bluff, even though he lived in Butler Springs.

If she agreed, good, bad, or ugly, her dinner date would be the lead story in the following day's gossip mill. Everyone would know she'd resorted to online dating to find a man, and not just any man, she wanted a soul mate. No matter how many times she told herself that dating apps were the norm nowadays, that everyone did it—heck, she'd even known of a few people who were practically addicted to the apps—deep down she still wanted her knight in shining armor to ride up on a powerful steed, single her out in a crowd, fall madly in love with her, and then sweep her off her feet.

"Don't you look pretty as a picture." For someone who had made an appointment to see the doc because she was feeling beyond poorly, Nadine Peabody stood by the front counter looking awfully chipper.

"Thank you." Even though Nora knew Nadine probably would have said that to anyone sitting by the front desk, she was nonetheless grateful for the small boost to her self esteem. "Feeling better?"

The woman's smile slid away and she reached for the nearby wall to brace herself. "Not really."

"Well, you take a seat and the doc will be with you shortly." Nora had no idea if the woman was putting on a brave face or fueling her own imagination. Either way it was her job to keep the patients comfortable until Brooks could see them.

"You are always so kind." Nadine shook her head and sighed. "I don't understand why some good man hasn't snatched you up yet. Smart *and* pretty women don't come along every day."

"That's sweet of you to say."

"Sweet my foot." Nadine leaned back in a waiting room chair and smiled. "Mark my words. One of these days someone with the sense God gave them is going to recognize you for the treasure you are and snap you right up."

Nora wasn't so sure that it was politically correct to refer to a woman as being snapped up by a man, but Nadine had a point. She was a catch and any man should be delighted to have her take interest in him. And so what if her knight in shining armor found her on the internet. There was no rule that said fate—or a pair of dogs—had to introduce a person to their soul mate.

Nodding her head, she reread the message she'd written. Her mom's voice repeating *if at first you don't succeed* played in her head. Maybe this time would be the charm. Or with her luck, *three strikes and you're out* would be more likely.

"There's been a slight change of plans."

Since Neil Farraday and his brothers had taken on this crazy reality television project, change of plans had become a regular part of his vocabulary. With only one episode under wraps, the overall plans for the rest of the season were good, and behind schedule. He did not need any more change of plans. “Describe slight.”

“Well.” His brother Owen cleared his throat. That was never a good sign. “The sisters were approached by a developer.”

Neil glanced at the dashboard clock. Tuckers Bluff was a bit more than thirty minutes ahead.

“Did you know that there are at least three abandoned homesteads—still standing, that is—just outside the city limits of Sadieville?”

“Can’t say that I did.” Nor did he see what that had to do with the network’s plans to refurbish a ghost town or why developers would be talking to the owners of the Sisters Boutique and Sadieville’s Parlor House.

“Even though only one episode has aired, the show is causing a lot of buzz.”

That much he knew. The network had been so excited with the reception for the *Ghost Town Fixer* episode they ran as a test, that they’d opted to change the series name in the event it ran for longer than the town had buildings. Promos had been blasting for the now renamed series—and boringly, if anyone asked him, not that they did—*The Construction Cousins*. Public reaction so far made the hype over Who Shot JR seem rather lackluster.

“Valerie on behalf of the production company, the sisters, a smattering of Farradays—”

“Including you?” It wasn’t really a question.

“Morgan, Ryan and me, along with the Tuckers Bluff City Council, had a meeting this morning over the future of Sadieville and the surrounding area. Making a long story short—”

If this was short, he didn’t want to hear the long version. At least not without a comfortable chair, tall beer, and some good music in the background. “Any chance you can make it even shorter? I’m almost in town.”

“Yeah. Based on the developers’ interest in Sadieville, Valerie and I pitched an idea. It was a hit. I went with Val and Morgan to check out one of Sadieville’s old houses. That’s when our beloved brother Morgan fell through the floor and scared the heck out of his wife. He’s got a broken ankle.”

"What! That should have led the conversation."

Owen chuckled. "I had a captive audience. No point in rushing."

"Comedian. How bad is the ankle?"

"Bad enough that Morgan won't be on his two feet wielding a hammer any time soon."

The clank of his college ring against the hard plastic of his steering wheel echoed in the small cab of his pickup. "Blast."

"Hope you brought your tool belt."

"Don't I always?" With this clan, pitching in wherever needed meant he was one of the few prominent architects he knew who wielded a hammer as often as he did a pencil.

"Good, because you've got until the film crew arrives next week to spit out the plans for the homestead remodel."

"Homestead? What happened to the hotel?" The plans he'd spent weeks drawing and re-drawing until everyone from the network and new owners to the producers and city council agreed. Mostly.

"That got shoved to later," Owen said. "The spa will be the episode after that. We'll also need—"

"Whatever it is, you can tell me in person. I'm coming up on the city limits."

"Fair enough. Have you eaten?"

"Yes, Mother."

"Not funny," Owen deadpanned. Their mother had been a bone of contention of late. She was none too happy that her sons were spending so much time in Tuckers Bluff. Which made no sense at all for a woman who had hammered into them that nothing was more important than family. "Morgan and Valerie are already installed at O'Fearadaigh's. Instead of following doctor's orders and going home to rest he's here, but at least his foot is propped up on a cushioned chair. I just slipped out to call you in peace and quiet."

"Okay. See you in a few."

"Later, bro."

The call disconnected and Neil took his time riding down Main Street. Like his cousins' family, the Oklahoma

Farradays had been cattle ranchers too, but over time, his branch of the clan veered off in a different direction. As the kids grew up and out of the cattle business, and it became clear not a single one was destined to follow in the family footsteps, his dad slowly sold the land off bit by bit, leased out some of the pastures to neighboring ranchers, and to the surprise of his family, started a Christmas tree farm on the remaining chunk of the land he'd kept for the family use. An even bigger surprise to everyone, especially his mother, had been that the idea actually reaped a profit every year.

His phone sounded again and he debated for a split second if he should send his mom to voice mail. He loved the woman as much as any son, maybe more, but she was not at all happy he was on his way back to Tuckers Bluff, and didn't seem to make any effort to hide her feelings. "Hi Mom."

"You there yet?"

"Just pulling into town."

A moment of silence hung. "I've tried calling your brothers. They've gone radio silent."

Crud. The question now was did he want to tell her about Morgan and the change of plans. He pulled his car into a spot in front of his cousin Jamison's pub. "Sorry Mom, I'm pulling into the pub now. I'll have Morgan or Owen call you."

"The pub," she scoffed. "Figures. Never mind. I'll talk to them tomorrow. Take care and hurry home."

"I'll do my best." A round of *I love you*'s was exchanged and Neil refrained from mentioning that the *slight change of plans* was going to keep him in Texas way longer than his mother would like. Of course, any time in Texas was more than his mother would like.

Stomping his feet on the hard concrete, he rolled his shoulders and neck before spotting the large furry dog by the side of the building staring at him. "Gray?" Slowly easing his way to where the Farraday cattle dog almost seemed to be standing guard like a gargoyle watchman, Neil held his hand out low and repeated the animal's name, relieved when the furry tail swished back and forth. "It is you. Who did you hitch a ride with and do they know you're here?" He took a minute to see if he recognized a ranch truck while scratching under the canine's chin. "I guess if you've waited this long you'll stay a bit longer." Stepping away, he yanked open the large wooden pub door and walked inside.

At just past the dinner hour, the place was already doing a fairly brisk business. Only a few tables remained empty. The music was loud enough to have a handful of couples on the dance floor, but low enough for most folks to be huddled in conversation. Except for one table. Off to the side, away from the majority of tables, a lone woman with shoulder length dark hair sat looking up at him. For a short moment their gazes met and even in this dim light, huge brown eyes drew him in and left him momentarily stunned like a deer in the proverbial headlights. A flash of disappointment sparked as she lowered her head, her hand slowly stroking a tall, almost empty beverage.

A variety of scenarios began running through his mind for what could have caused such a pretty woman to nurse a drink alone in a family run pub. Most had his brows creasing with distaste.

"If you're looking for your brothers, they're in the opposite corner." Abbie, Jamison's wife and occasional hostess, bumped shoulders with him.

He couldn't bring himself to pull his gaze away from the brunette, but leaned into his in-law and lowered his voice. "What's that gal's story?"

It took Abbie a few moments for her gaze to settle in the same direction. "Nora?"

This time he turned to make sure she was looking at the same person he was before he nodded.

"Not sure." She frowned. "I got the impression she was waiting for someone, but she's been here for just over an hour and is still nursing the same drink. If I didn't know better, I'd say she was stood up."

"Know better how?"

"For one thing, I can't remember the last time I saw her out on a date."

"Really?" That made no sense to him at all.

Abbie nodded. "Nice girls often aren't the popular ones. That aside, if she had a date with someone here in Tuckers Bluff, *anyone* here in Tuckers Bluff, trust me when I say half the town would have known about it before she did. And they'd have been talking about it all day too, bless her heart."

In the last few months he'd spent enough time at his uncle's ranch to know that Abbie was most definitely not exaggerating. "Tell my brothers I'll be over in a bit. Oh, and whoever rode in tonight from the ranch, let them know Gray is out front."

"Gray?" Abbie sighed. "He must be roaming again. If he's still there when you leave, you might want to give him a lift."

"Sure." Following Abbie's unconcerned lead over the dog, his gaze darted to the brunette, Nora, and back to his cousin's wife.

Abbie studied him for a second before hefting one shoulder in a lazy shrug and turning on her heel. He had about five seconds to make up his mind and with one foot moving in front of the other and the distance between him and the brunette growing shorter, he was pretty sure his mind had been made up in two. The next question was whether or not that decision was the smartest or dumbest thing he'd ever done.

CHAPTER TWO

This was why Nora didn't want to date in Tuckers Bluff, and why she should have stuck to her guns and insisted on meeting candidate number four anywhere less public. When she'd walked up to the pub and spotted Gray standing guard by the corner of the building, she briefly considered the folklore and almost let herself believe this new match would be golden. Instead, here she sat alone, and by tomorrow morning the whole town would figure out she'd been stood up about five minutes after her friends worked out that she'd tried online dating.

"Sorry I'm late." The tall, dark-haired man who had just come through the front door greeted her a little more loudly than was necessary for anyone who wasn't hard of hearing.

"Excuse me?" It had only taken her a second after the catalogue-worthy man had removed his hat by the front door to realize he wasn't the nice face she'd seen on her screen.

"The drive took longer than I'd thought and you know how cell service is, or isn't, in these parts." He slid into the seat across from her and leaning forward, lowered his voice so only she could hear. "Ma'am, I hope you're not going to skin me alive but you look like a lady in need of some company. Should I stay, or go sit with my brothers?"

Brothers? Her gaze quickly surveyed the surrounding tables landing on a familiar group of smiling men and then flickered back to the face in front of her. Strong chiseled features, deep blue eyes, wavy dark hair. Of course. A Farraday. And along with the handsome genes that stretched across all branches of the Irish clan, chivalry ran strong in their veins as well. A wave of relief washed over her. She wasn't sure if it was because she didn't have to make a scene brushing off a lunatic, or that she wouldn't have to explain to half the town why she'd been sitting alone at O'Fearadaigh's tonight. Either way she put on a pleasant smile. "Feel free to sit." A small voice in the back of her head scolded her. *What a pathetic move. Are you that desperate?* Scrambling, she quickly added, "For a minute."

"Thank you. Have you eaten? I'm starving." Her knight in shining armor bestowed that wide knee-melting smile that all the Farradays were famous for. Not waiting for her to respond, he flagged down a waitress before facing her again. "I should probably introduce myself. Neil—"

"Farraday," she finished for him.

"Have we met?" A deep line formed between buckled brows.

She shook her head. "Anyone who has grown up in this town can spot a Farraday a mile away. Even those of you from Oklahoma."

"I see."

"How can I help you?" A waitress Nora didn't recognize smiled at them.

"Do you have any corned beef left?"

The waitress beamed and nodded. "Absolutely."

"Great." He turned to Nora. "What would you like?"

She considered mentioning she'd not told him she was hungry, but as luck would have it she was starving and figured like letting him sit down, ordering dinner would draw less attention to her. "I'll have a Reuben sandwich with the sweet potato tots."

"Sounds delicious. I'll have the same. Also, bring us a piece of the apple rhubarb pie. Two forks." Clearly her surprise must have shown on her face because he chuckled and turned his hands palm up in front of him. "Life is short, might as well have dessert first. Besides, my brief experience with dinner here is that the pie runs out early."

He had a point. On two counts. What better way to right an evening with a miserable start than with a delicious dessert? And all the desserts tended to run out early.

"If you want to, though, we could eat the dessert later."

She shook her head. "About now, starting with dessert sounds like heaven." What woman didn't want warm delicious comfort food after a day like hers?

"Exactly what I was thinking." He leaned forward and lowered his voice. "I'm really glad you didn't throw me overboard, so to speak. My brothers are going to want to talk work and I desperately need fuel before I deal with them."

"Glad I could be of help," she whispered back. This guy was very much a Farraday. He had bailing out a damsel in distress down pat. It would have been so easy to start with what was a nice girl like her doing alone in a place like this—not that here wasn't a nice place—instead he spun the situation into her rescuing him. "I thought all you Oklahoma Farradays lived and breathed rebuilding the world one project at a time. What's so unpleasant it has you rescuing strangers on an empty stomach?" She flashed a smile to soften her words.

"I'm not sure that it is—yet. But if you'll excuse me a minute, I'd like to wash my hands before the food arrives."

"Sure thing."

She kept her gaze on his back as he disappeared down the rear hall, then pretended not to be staring after him when he made his way back to the table.

"So," Neil leaned back in his seat, "where were we?"

"Not wanting to talk shop with your brothers."

He nodded. "You're right about one thing. I can't imagine working with anyone but my brothers, as you say, one project at time. Although too often we're juggling way more than that at once. Only this time they threw a curveball at me and I've got to do about a month's worth of work in a few days."

"Ouch. How so?"

"The new reality show they've been working on is shifting gears. Rather than using the plans I've drawn up for the hotel, we're working on an old homestead now."

"Ah, so you're the vision behind the group?"

"I don't know about that, but I wield a mean pencil."

That made her laugh. Much to her surprise, she was

actually glad her original date was a no show.

The pie arrived and she almost felt guilty digging in before having dinner. Fork in hand, she stabbed at the flaky crust and took a small bite. "Oh wow. This is way better than I expected."

"You've not had it before?"

She shook her head. "Honestly, I don't eat here very often and when I do, I rarely include dessert." No point telling him being over thirty years old, calories had a way of bypassing the digestive process and going straight for her hips. "But trust me, this will be corrected."

"Smart woman," he chuckled, stabbing at another bite.

Even though she'd gobbled up more than her share, when the sandwiches arrived she was surprised to discover she was still famished. One bite and just like the pie, she almost groaned with delight. "I swear there's magic in their corned beef pot."

"No arguments from me. Though I'm more inclined to believe they've got fairies working in that kitchen."

"Agreed. And the baked goods fairy is named Antoinette." She popped a tater tot into her mouth. "Tell me more about the new project."

Through bites and sips of his drink, he told her what he knew. "I'll know more after I chat with the others."

"Older homes can be so much fun. Aren't you just a little excited at the prospect of bringing a house like that back to life?"

"That depends."

"On what?"

"How good that centenarian's bones are. If she's as good as the buildings in town, yeah." He grinned a little bit. "It could be a lot of fun, but no matter what, it's going to be a lot of work. For all I know the place may not even have electricity."

"Ooh," she set the last bit of her sandwich down on her plate, "I hadn't thought about that."

"Running water could be another issue."

Suddenly her mind ran to those graphics on Facebook asking if you had no internet or TV could you live in a cabin for a month. Her first thought had always gone to what about running water, heat, and bathrooms. "Will your brothers have all these answers?"

"Maybe, but I plan to see for myself as soon as possible."

"I wonder how good or bad it is. Sometimes houses that old are just as interesting because of who lived there and what happened in them as they are because of the architectural features."

"You sound like you have some experience."

She chuckled. "As much as I can get watching television shows about refurbishing old homes or tracing family history. How soon do you think you'll get to go look?"

"First light." He snapped his fingers. "Forgot tomorrow's Sunday. I'll have to get my first look after church."

She didn't have the heart to tell him that missing out on Sunday dinner was probably more sacrilegious to the heads of the Farraday clan than skipping church. Of course, if he were her family, she could forgive this man anything.

Neil knew he really should go seek out his family, but he didn't want to leave Nora. Not that he was being noble or anything, he was truly enjoying himself. At least he'd had the good sense early on to excuse himself and seek out his cousin's wife. Abbie was the only person in the place who knew he wasn't the date Nora had been waiting for and he preferred if it remained that way.

"Hey, little brother." Ryan stepped up to the table and slapped him on the back. "We're heading back to the ranch. Don't want Aunt Eileen waiting up for us."

"Sorry, I should have told you I was meeting Nora for dinner."

"No problem." He could see his brother casually glancing in Nora's direction. "Nice to see you again."

Neil blinked. How did his brother know her and he didn't?

"Same here. Are you and your brothers going to be staying longer this visit?" Nora smiled politely at Ryan and Neil was struck by the way her eyes sparkled. He probably should have spent more time in Tuckers Bluff during the mercantile project than he did.

"Not sure yet," Ryan shrugged, "but it's starting to look that way."

"You coming or you planning on joining them for dessert?" Paxton came up beside Ryan.

"If you need to go…" Nora moved her napkin from her lap to beside her empty plate.

"No." He skewered his brothers with a leave-us-alone glare. "There's no hurry."

"No, ma'am. None at all," Ryan spoke as he took a step back, nudging his brother with an elbow. "See you later, Neil."

A few more seconds and his brothers fell into behaving as if they were teens again. They nudged, shoved, and tussled each other out the pub door.

"You really don't have to stay. You've done your good deed for the day. We can leave if you need to go."

"Good deed sounds so unpleasant. I've really enjoyed the company. Thank you."

"Saying you're welcome doesn't make sense when I'm the one who needed rescuing."

He very much wanted to ask her rescuing from what, but fear of embarrassing her helped him keep his mouth shut.

Using her straw to stir a near empty glass of soda, she glanced at him over the rim. "Aren't you going to ask?"

There was no point in pretending he didn't understand the question. "I'm a little curious what idiot left you here alone."

"Okay," she grinned, "that is the nicest way to describe getting stood up I've ever heard."

"So who's the idiot?"

She shrugged. "No one special. I met him online and we

were supposed to meet for the first time tonight."

"Looks like you dodged a bullet."

Her eyes narrowed with confusion.

"Clearly if he's too rude to let you know he can't make it, he's not only an idiot, he's not good enough for you. Hence, you dodged a bullet."

"I dodged two."

"Two?"

"The first, as you so kindly pointed out, I managed to avoid getting involved with an idiot. The second, thanks to you, I've avoided being the center of gossip for being stood up. Which would have made even juicier fodder on the grapevine once I explained that I met the idiot online." Her gaze dropped to the drink as she continued to stir, then once again looked up. "Maybe now I can stall having to tell people that I've resorted to online dating."

"Lots of people do it."

"Stall?" She smiled at him.

"Do online dating. Those apps for connecting with people near you or who are similar in some way or other are as popular as social media and video streaming. Not that video streaming has anything to do with dating, but you can see what I mean."

"I know, but the old fashioned gal in me just isn't comfortable sharing that yet."

Considering he'd thought the idea of meeting someone to get close and personal with in such a distant and impersonal way a distasteful concept, he couldn't blame her for not wanting to share that information. If he were being honest with himself, she was braver than him to even give it a try.

"Are you going to try again?"

"I'll be. It's true." A tall willowy blonde who could probably walk with a book on her head paused beside their table.

"Hi Emily." From the way Nora's spine stiffened, he'd guess she wasn't all that happy to see Emily. "This is a surprise."

"Being Saturday night and all, we decided to pop by for

a little music and dancing after dinner at the café. Heard you had a date tonight. Thought old Burt from the hardware store had gotten his wires crossed." Her gaze shifted to Neil then back. "Nice to meet you…."

Her words hung a long moment when he realized she was waiting for his name. "Neil."

"You're a Farraday, aren't you?" Her tone didn't hint at whether the words were meant as a compliment or accusation.

"Yes ma'am." What more could he say.

The man Emily came in with nudged her by the elbow. "We'd better grab that last table unless you want to stand all night."

Emily turned her attention back to Nora. "Better not let this one get away. After all, you're not getting any younger."

If the backhanded dig wasn't enough, the stiff smile on Nora's face told him all he needed to know about this lady. He waited until Emily was out of earshot. "If all the gossips in town are like that, I see what you mean about not wanting to deal with the grapevine."

"When it comes to spreading juicy gossip about anyone's short comings, Emily Taub gives visualization to the old adage *telegraph, telephone and tell a woman*. She feeds on the misfortunes of others. Especially if it's even the tiniest bit embarrassing."

"Why do I not find that hard to believe." Though he was now more curious as to what Emily meant by that last departing crack, and more concerned with how she'd spin what she'd seen tonight. "Would I be winning any bets if I were to guess that your letting *this one* get away would make her all too happy to have something to gossip about?"

Rolling her eyes, Nora let out a less than amused chuckle. "Emily dated Adam his senior year of high school. She was the reason the Farraday men developed the policy of never dating women from close to home. Some folks say she never got over letting a Farraday slip through her fingers, but likes having the title of the only woman from town, before Becky, to get even close to a Farraday. Too many people in this town live for something to gossip about. It'll never change. That's why I wanted to keep my private life private."

"From Emily?"

Reluctantly, she bobbed her head. "Emily was one of the popular girls. Always had a guy on her arm and always looked down on those who didn't."

"And you were…?"

"One who didn't. My freshman year I got friendly with one of the popular boys. We chatted at the lockers, occasionally grabbed lunch together, that sort of thing. It was very flattering to have an upperclassman be nice to me. I even thought he might ask me to the prom."

"But…"

"Emily. She was always very flirtatious, very social, and easily managed to turn my friend's head. Eventually she dumped him for Adam. It's been a lot of years, but she and everyone else in town know my dating life has had a very long dry spell. You could say I fit the bill, lucky in cards unlucky in love."

Which would explain the parting crack about not getting any younger. Every school in every town had the popular crowd, the not so popular, the jocks, the geeks, the brainiacs, and of course, the mean girls. It rubbed him very much the wrong way that Emily was already gloating. "I have an idea."

The hand stirring the drink stilled and her brows lifted high on her forehead.

"Don't look at me that way, it's not a bad idea. What if—just to make this little dinner date have a little more bite to it—what if we did this again a time or two? Then you can dump me."

Nora stared a long moment and pressed her lips tightly into a smile. "That would certainly give her something to talk about."

"What do you say?"

"You don't have to do that. She'll forget all about my surprise date as soon as some poor soul says or does something stupid that she can spread around town like manure on a windy day."

He tried not to cringe at the image. "You're probably right about that. And you're absolutely right that I don't *have to* continue this little charade." He let his words hang.

The way she seemed to mull his words over told him she had at least one reason for wanting to put one over on one Emily Taub.

"Up to you," he continued. "We can walk away tonight and you can tell your friends that you really can't stand the way I eat a sandwich." He smiled and hoped that put her at ease.

Nora's gaze settled on the front door, her jaw tightening moments before she blurted, "Lord love a duck. Did they tell the whole town?"

He did his casual best to glance over his shoulder at a group of women huddled by the front door, looking in their direction and whispering back and forth. He had no idea who they were, but obviously Nora did and she wasn't happy about it.

Lips pressed tightly together, she gave a curt nod. "Deal."

"What?" He'd almost forgotten what they were talking about. Almost.

"One or two more dates. That should do it."

He raised his glass to hers and grinned. "Deal."

CHAPTER THREE

Whether in Tuckers Bluff or back home, attending Sunday morning services had been a part of Neil's life for as long as he could remember. Truth be told, some Sundays he paid more attention than others. Most of the weekly sermons in his teenage years had been a blur. His mind had usually been on girls, or cars, or how to improve his game, whatever the season might have been. Today, he might as well have been a teenager again. His mind darted back and forth from Nora sitting across the center aisle, to the pull of his steering wheel on the ride into town this morning, and of course, the ghost town project.

"You still with us, dude?" Morgan balanced on his crutches with their Aunt Eileen and Uncle Sean to one side and Neil at the other.

"Sorry. Just thinking."

"About the homestead, I hope."

"What else?" He truly hoped Morgan wasn't about to venture guesses on what had really been on his mind because the answers could prove to be a little embarrassing.

"Come up with anything good?"

"Would you give the guy a break." Owen walked up and slapped him on the shoulder. "It hasn't even been twenty-four hours since we dumped this on him."

"I know, but the city council needs our numbers."

Their uncle bobbed his head. "That may be true but they're not unreasonable. This project isn't like updating our hall bathroom. They'll wait for you to get your math done, and done fairly for everyone."

More of his Farraday cousins and their wives meandered over. Declan and Brooks lingered by the church doors with a few parishioners Neil didn't recognize. Not that that was any surprise. He'd spent enough time in town to get to know quite a few people, but not nearly enough to recognize most of the natives. Except for one. Nora laughed over something one of the three women she stood with had said, then patted the friend's arm gently and turned to walk in their direction.

As soon as Nora got within listening distance, Aunt Eileen waved her closer. "Will you be joining us for supper today? I've got my cola pot roast in the oven."

"That's not playing fair," Nora teased. "I've got a long list of chores I'm supposed to be doing, but you know how much I love your pot roast."

Aunt Eileen rolled back on her heels and grinned merrily. "Yes. I surely do."

"About supper," Neil interrupted. "Do you think I have time to run out to the homestead first? I need to take a closer look, get some measurements, a few pictures. The sooner I do that the sooner I'll have answers for my impatient brothers and the town council."

"Sure, as long as you're back before the sun sets."

He pivoted around to face Nora. They were supposed to put on a bit of a show for the town and since she liked old houses, now seemed as good a time as any to start. Though this probably wouldn't count as a real date, who was he to nitpick. "Would you like to join me for a ride?"

"To the homestead?" Her eyes beamed. "I'd love it."

"Then we have a plan." Aunt Eileen nodded at Nora. "You might as well leave your car at your place. One of the boys can bring you home after supper when they come back to town."

"I don't want to put anyone out."

"Nonsense." Aunt Eileen waved the objection away with a smile.

"As usual, Aunt Eileen is right." Adam stood the closest to hear the conversation. "Any of us coming home after supper will be glad to bring you back."

Nora nodded and Neil wanted to say there'd be no need for his cousins to get involved. If he brought her to supper, he could take her home. Fortunately, if he'd learned one thing through the years it was not to argue with his aunt. They'd do it her way—for now.

A few more minutes of after-church chit chat and Nora excused herself to go home to park her car. As quickly as he could extricate himself from the family dynamic, Neil followed right behind her. He'd barely pulled in front of the veterinarian clinic and her second floor apartment when she came bouncing down the stairs, her Sunday dress replaced by jeans and boots, and holding a bottle of water in each hand.

"That was fast."

"When you share a sorority house with fifteen women and only three bathrooms, you learn to expedite hair and makeup. Or in my case not bother at all." Nora shrugged and tossed him a bottle. "Afternoons get pretty warm this time of year."

"Thank you." If he'd been more focused this morning it would've occurred to him to pack drinks and snacks in case his first walk-through took longer than expected.

"I've also got some of Toni's glazed donuts in my bag."

"When did you find time to grab those?"

"Easy. What folks don't eat during the early coffee time, the parishioners get to take with them. I always scope out Toni's leftovers."

"Smart woman." He slammed the car door and circled around to the driver's side.

"The hard part is resisting the temptation to nibble during the sermon."

"I've had Toni's desserts. If her donuts are just as good then you're a stronger person than me. I'd have eaten them all, sermon or no sermon."

She threw her head back and laughed. "I don't know about that. You don't look like you have a willpower problem."

"Don't count on it." Only he wasn't thinking about donuts.

The homestead was a decent length drive outside of town. Far enough that he was having a hard time wrapping his head around why the town or developers would want to invest the kind of money that would be needed to not only revitalize the old ghost town as a tourist attraction but also turn it into a viable option for full time residents.

"I'm really glad you invited me." She unscrewed the cap from the water bottle. "I love looking at houses. We don't move a ton of real estate around here, but whenever there's an open house I always make time to look. And like I mentioned last night, I love all the remodeling shows on TV, not just the old house ones."

"A lot of people seem to love remodeling shows on TV."

"What's not to love? You walk into an ordinary house just like the ones we ordinary mortals live in and when they're done you're strolling through the pages of a magazine shoot. All the thrills without emptying your own bank account."

"Well, that could explain why the networks are going bananas over this new show we've gotten ourselves into."

"You say that like it's a bad thing."

"It's not a bad thing, it actually has potential to be quite profitable for us. Right after the pilot episode was aired our phones back home rang off the hook."

"I understand you've had a lot of interest from folks around these parts as well."

He nodded. "I'm not sure we can handle much more interest. At least not if we want to keep this a small family business."

She spun sideways in the seat to better face him, her eyes rounded almost with what he'd say was alarm. "But y'all are going to finish bringing Sadieville back to life?"

"Absolutely. Valerie is family now."

"And Farradays always take care of family."

He smiled at her. "That about covers it."

"Oh," she sat up straighter, "there it is. I haven't been to see Sadieville since y'all fixed up the Mercantile."

"Except we don't have time for visiting this afternoon." Glancing at his GPS he turned right at the next dirt road. The years had taken their toll on the path to the few remaining homesteads. "According to Morgan, he and Paxton chose the most stable home for the project."

Nora's gaze narrowed as she and he focused on a blur in the distance. A gray wood clapboard structure that was doing little to inspire optimism. "Oh…boy." Seatbelt undone before he'd fully stopped, she was out of the car before he could get to her door. "Y'all are going to turn this into a magazine?"

"That's the plan." He was willing to admit so far this old home was not love at first sight. On the other hand, of all the things he'd ever done, this would by far be the most interesting challenge. If it didn't fall down around them first.

From the looks of the old house, she wasn't all that sure she wanted to step onto the porch, never mind go inside. The house was definitely teetering left and she was fairly confident there were more shingles on the ground than the roof. "Your brothers are sure this is the best of the bunch?"

"That's what they said, and my brother Paxton is one of the best structural engineers I know." His gaze scanned the front from one side to the other and she wondered if perhaps he was reconsidering his brother's skill set.

"Don't suppose you have any hard hats in that truck? You might need them."

"Afraid not. You'd better let me go in first."

"Like police in a raid. Make sure there's no boogieman hiding in the closet."

He chuckled under his breath. "Something like that."

She took a step back. "I'll wait for you to shout out the all clear signal. Do you need a gun?" She flashed a toothy grin and patted her middle. "I have one if you need it."

One brow raised, his gaze dropped to her midsection.

"You don't have to look at me like that. I wasn't about to take any chances. Not only have I lived in West Texas my entire life, I heard all the stories about Joanna and the snakes in this town."

"Got it. All the same, unless we hear a very loud rattle, I'd prefer you kept your weapon concealed."

"Okay." She took a step back and watched him carefully test the porch before taking each step.

He'd only been inside a couple of minutes when he called out to her. "All clear!"

"I know you're an architect." She gingerly tested the first, then second step onto the porch. "But are you qualified as an engineer?" Inside there was no sign of him. She took her time crossing what she guessed was the living room, taking a moment to look up at the *au naturel* sunlight—a.k.a. hole in the ceiling—and circumventing a smaller hole in the middle of the floor. No doubt where Morgan had broken his ankle. She was less than impressed. "Hello?"

"I'm in the kitchen." A small square apparatus in hand, Neil held it against the wall, and then jotted something down onto a pad of paper. "Just measuring the rooms."

"Even measuring tapes have gone Star Trek on us." With every passing day she was convinced that she would probably live long enough to one day be beamed up to the mothership.

His phone replacing the techno measurer, Neil snapped a few photos in every direction. Standing in a small square area with a splattering of crooked cabinets and a few doors hanging by a single hinge, what she figured had to be the kitchen came sans appliances.

"I was kind of hoping to find an original stove. Depending on when the place was abandoned, maybe even an icebox."

"Oh." Her mind flashed to her grandmother's ancient kitchen. "You know what else? One of those old cast iron sinks that spread out on either side like a countertop with ridges for drying dishes to drain back into the sink."

"Exactly. A truly original farm sink. Old can be really cool in the right setting."

While she had a clear picture in mind of her grandma's sink, she couldn't see a whole lot of cool in this room. As soon as he finished measuring one room, he continued to another and she followed close behind. Every so often he'd stop, cross his arms, his gaze slowly moving back and forth intently before he'd nod, snap a few photos, and move on.

They'd weaved their way through multiple areas when it struck her that something was missing. "Where's the bathroom?"

Neil stopped in his tracks as if the thought hadn't occurred to him and walked down the narrow hallway popping his head into a small closet. "Now that you mention it, older homes weren't big on closets. I bet this is the bathroom."

Her gaze bounced from corner to corner. Nothing about this room looked like it had ever had anything close to running water. "I don't know."

"Bathroom as in where the bathtub was. I have a feeling the toilet was somewhere in the backyard and bedroom washstands were still the norm. Though it's wired for electrical so," he shrugged, "who knows. When I'm done here I'll check around the yard and see if I can find any signs of an old outhouse."

The thought actually gave her a shiver. "I can not even begin to imagine having to stomp out in the freezing winter in the dead of night to use an outhouse."

"Most folks probably kept a pan under the bed and used the outhouse in the day time."

"Okay, that doesn't make me feel any better."

A low rumble of laughter erupted. "I hear you."

She'd taken a heavier step to spin around and exit the supposed bathroom when a crackling sound echoed around them and Neil reached out looping his arms around her just as the floorboard underneath gave way.

"Careful. You all right?"

One foot in a hole in the ground and one up on the bathroom floor, she wasn't sure what she was. "I don't think I broke anything. Can you help me up?"

Gingerly, his hands around her waist, he leveraged her up and out of the hole, steadying her beside him. "I think we've done enough measuring and exploring for one day."

"Mm." Her mind had gone momentarily blank.

Regardless that Neil had taken hold of her to prevent her from breaking a bone like his brother, or worse, her neck, it had been a long time since she'd felt a man's strong hands anywhere. As far as knights in shining armors went, two for two, so far Neil Farraday was doing a great job of rescuing her. She kind of liked that. Almost enough to see about falling through the floor somewhere else in the house. Then again, maybe she'd just wait and see how else her knight in shining armor might catch her.

CHAPTER FOUR

"Cut." Eileen Farraday passed the deck of cards to Ruth Ann on her left.

"I know. I'm just saying, it's a little fishy that for all these years not hide nor hair of Patrick and his family and now, one by one, all those boys are here in town more than back home in Oklahoma."

Dorothy picked up her first card. "Doesn't seem fishy to me. It's because of that TV show."

"She's right." Sally May waved a thumb at Dorothy. "Who wouldn't want their own TV show?"

Three hands popped up and Sally May let her hands drop to the table. "You're kidding?"

Eileen lifted her attention from the cards in her hands. "Why anyone would want cameras and microphones following them around all the time is beyond me."

"Not to mention," Ruth Ann closed her cards, "all the *people* dealing with the cameras and microphones."

"Not a minute of privacy." Dorothy tossed a chip into the kitty.

"But this is different." Sally May picked up her cards again. "This is just filming their work place, not their personal lives. A nine to five gig and voila, they're famous."

"And who wants to be famous?" Anyone who'd known Eileen decades ago would have been more than a little shocked to hear those words coming out of her mouth. Once upon a time that had been exactly her dream. Now she wouldn't trade her life for all the fame and fortune in the world.

"Yoo hoo." Ruth Ann snapped her fingers. "Are you in?"

"Oh." Eileen tossed a chip into the pot. "I was just thinking."

"About Patrick and his brother?" The hopeful look in Ruth Ann's eyes almost made Eileen laugh.

She really didn't have a clue what had happened to cause the rift between the Texas and Oklahoma Farradays. All she knew is one day they were all one big happy family, and the next they weren't.

Ruth Ann set two cards on the table. "I'll take two. And for what it's worth, it's kind of nice having more Farraday eye candy around."

"I'll second that." Sally May rearranged the cards in her hand. "If I weren't too old and—"

"Too married," three voices echoed.

"Well." Sally May huffed. "It's true."

Dorothy grinned. "Nora's not too old."

"And certainly not too married," Ruth Ann added.

Dorothy shifted her cards. "They do look really cute. I was at the Cut N Curl for a trim this morning and Polly told me they were awfully cozy at the pub Saturday night."

Ruth Ann pressed her cards to her chest and leaned into the table. "I heard they've been dating for a while and keeping it secret."

"Grapevine says he's getting ready to propose." Sally May nodded. "Supposedly, that's why they're going public."

"Anyone ready for a refill?" Abbie stood by Eileen's side, coffee pot in hand. "And who's about to propose?"

"Neil," Sally May answered.

Abbie's jaw popped open. "To who?"

Three voices chorused. "Nora."

Sally May continued, "I have it from a reliable source that they've been hot and heavy since the pilot was filmed and are coming out now."

"Uh." Abbie's head whipped around to face Eileen.

Her mind replayed yesterday's happenings in the churchyard and then over supper. Adam and Meg had given Nora a lift home. Surely if there was something more going on, Neil would have insisted on making the round trip. Then again, the two of them did seem to have a connection of some sort, but hot and heavy weren't the first words to come to mind. "I don't think so."

"Don't think what?" Ruth Ann looked up. "That he's getting ready to propose?"

"Actually, no." Eileen folded her cards in her hand. "I don't. He does seem a bit smitten, but I think the grapevine may be ahead of themselves on this one."

"I agree." Abbie nodded and managed a weak smile. "I think this might be another case of the grapevine overreacting."

"Speak of the devil." Sally May's smile took over her face.

Neil stood momentarily at the café doorway, glancing around before striding toward them. "Hello ladies. Aunt Eileen." He leaned over and kissed her cheek.

"Taking a break?" she asked her nephew.

"Yeah. Got an early start." He faced Abbie. "Do you mind if I park it in one of your corner tables? I'm getting really tired of my own coffee."

"Sure thing. Take your pick but the tables by the back door fill up last."

"Sounds good. I've done the bulk of the plans in the office upstairs but I think we need a new coffee pot."

Abbie smiled. "Have you eaten anything today?"

Neil's eyes widened and then he chuckled. "Now that you mention it, I did skip breakfast."

"And whose fault is that?" Eileen glared at her nephew. He'd been in an all fired hurry to get to the apartment over the café. The cousins had been using it for an office since they'd taken on so much work in Tuckers Bluff along with the ghost town project.

"All on me." He held up a long scroll of what Eileen suspected were the plans for the homestead project. "I'd better get back to work. See y'all later."

Yeah. And once she wasn't surrounded by the Ladies Afternoon Social Club, she had a few questions for him.

Some mornings Nora wished that she could just consume her caffeine intravenously. Today was one of those mornings. Practically from the moment she walked in the front door, long before office hours, phones had been ringing off the hook and patients had been filing in without appointments. It hadn't helped any that Brooks had been delayed by an emergency at the hospital. She'd rearranged as many appointments as she could and once Brooks made it into the office she'd switched hats from receptionist extraordinaire to family practioner's nurse. She'd taken blood pressures, temperatures, changed bandages, and with the effort and determination of a military invasion, by two o'clock they were almost caught up. Of course skipping lunch had probably had a lot to do with it. Though she wasn't going to complain. She preferred hectic days like this with chaotic schedules and simple cases. The days when all hell broke loose for more critical reasons and no matter how hard she and Brooks tried, they'd either lose a patient or deliver a miserable diagnosis, those kind of days always ate a little at her soul.

She tapped on the door frame of his office. "I'm thinking Frank's meatball parmesan on warm bread would hit the spot right about now."

"Oh, that does sound good. I think I burned up that yogurt you gave me about two hours ago."

"Great, because I already phoned in the order."

Brooks laughed from deep in his belly. "What would I ever do without you?"

"Aren't you glad I'm not planning on giving you a chance to find out?"

"That's not what I'm hearing." Brooks leaned back in his chair and crossed his arms. "Mrs. Martin spent every minute of her appointment with me letting me know that you and my cousin Neil should be running off to get married anytime now."

"Oh, really?" She grinned at him. Only someone who

had known Brooks as long as she had would recognize the twinkle in his eyes that belied the stern look on his face. Meg, Adam's wife, had been one of those early morning phone calls wanting to know what had she missed to spark all the gossip. Nora had done all she could, short of telling the truth, to convince one of her dearest friends that for now there was nothing more than a little casual flirtation going on with her and the Farraday cousin. She was glad to be able to simply play with Brooks over the rumors. "I'd better check my calendar. Wouldn't want to be otherwise occupied."

Brooks leaned forward again and smiled. "I assured Mrs. Martin, and everyone else who brought up the subject, that if there were any truth to the rumors I'd be sure to let them know."

"Everyone?"

"Well, almost everyone."

Who knew a little visit in the pub and a family dinner could spark so many imaginations. What was she saying. She'd lived in Tuckers Bluff her whole life. Of course she knew that a smile was all anyone had needed for generations to start rumors. "I'd better go get us some sustenance before your next appointment arrives. By the sheer grace of God you've had two back to back cancellations and no more walk-ins. I'll run over and pick up the order. You take a break."

"Thanks."

The good thing about living in a small town was that residents could get almost anywhere within walking distance. That included a five minute walk from Brooks' offices to the café. On nice days like today, the walk was an appreciated change of pace.

"Your order's almost ready," Abbie called to her from the register as soon as she'd crossed the threshold. "We got in a busload of tourists a bit ago and we've been running a bit crazy. Aunt Eileen had to pitch in again."

"No hurry. Thanks." Looking around, she immediately spotted the ladies playing cards. Even though they were all old enough to be her mother, and in Dorothy's case, almost old enough to be her grandmother, when time allowed she'd enjoyed playing with them on Saturday mornings. Despite the age gaps, they were a lot of fun. Occasionally even a bit crazy, but fun.

Two steps in the direction of the ladies and she noticed Abbie almost twitching, gesturing with her head to the other side of the café. Tucked in a rear corner on two tables pushed together, Neil was absorbed in the paperwork in front of him. Taking a second look at the ladies engrossed in their card game, she pivoted and headed over to Neil. After all, the gossip mill was running at full speed, a little more fuel wouldn't change much.

Almost at the table, Neil looked up and smiled at her. "This is a nice surprise."

"Ditto. It's been a crazy day at the office and this is our first chance to break for lunch."

Neil dropped his pencil on papers spread over the table.

"Designs for the house yesterday?" She inched closer, looking over his shoulder.

"Yes." His face lit up. "I had to think on it a bit, but it's coming along nicely."

She did her best to discern the spaces and wasn't having much success. "You sure we're looking at the same house?"

"I am." He chuckled softly. "We're of course moving walls. The trick is modern appeal while keeping the craftsman charm."

"That old house is craftsman?"

"For the most part." He nodded. "Once it's cleaned up and restored it will be more obvious."

"Lunch is ready," Abbie called from the counter.

"Thanks."

"Listen, I have to make a run to a warehouse this side of Butler Springs. See what they have in stock since everyone is in a hurry to move forward. Want to tag along?"

How big of an idiot was he? Who in their right mind invited

a pretty woman to go digging through building supply warehouses? "Never mind, that sort of thing is probably boring to you."

"Depending on when you're going, sounds like fun." Her expression reflected sincerity, not a polite response. "The only time I could go is tomorrow. Tuesday is the day Brooks does house calls for folks who can't make it into town."

"House calls? And he hasn't been drummed out of the AMA?"

She chuckled. "Shh."

He smiled back at her. House calls was just one more reminder of how old school Tuckers Bluff really was. Even in his small part of Oklahoma, doctors simply didn't care for patients outside of their office or a hospital. Then again, he wasn't sure if there was anywhere else in Texas outside of Farraday country where doctors made house calls. "Tomorrow is perfect. Is nine too early?"

"Considering our first patients usually start arriving at eight, nine is like sleeping in on a Saturday."

"Yoo hoo," Abbie called again. "Do I need to stick these under the warmer?"

"No. I'm coming." She turned to him. "See you tomorrow."

He nodded, keeping his eyes on her as she paid for the order and hurried out the door. He'd barely returned his attention to the work in front of him when the sound of approaching boot heels made him look up. Not that he didn't already know who it was. "Hey, Aunt Eileen."

"Mind if I sit down a minute?"

"Of course not." He really didn't mind; he loved his aunt, but he also knew even if he'd said no, she still would have spoken her mind. "What's up?"

"Funny, that's what I was going to ask you."

For a moment he considered playing dumb, but he knew what she and most of the town wanted to know. "Not much. Working on this new project, the crew is arriving in a couple of days and I'm supposed to have plans ready to go."

"That was not what I was asking about."

“I know. I was getting to that part. Nora is coming with me tomorrow to source supplies.”

His aunt leaned back in her chair smiling. “How much of these rumors should I be paying attention to?”

He shook his head. “None of it. We are just getting to know each other.”

“I see.” His aunt pushed away from the table and leaned over to kiss him on the cheek and whispered in his ear, “She’s a nice girl.”

He already knew that.

CHAPTER FIVE

Nine o'clock rolled around faster than Nora had expected. She'd never had a problem sleeping, but last night she'd alternated between dreaming of dogs and wolves playing around in a large field with lots of puppies, to tossing and turning and staring at the clock. Somewhere around six she'd fallen back into a deep sleep and crazy dreams only to drag herself out of bed in order to be ready in time.

She'd barely scarfed down an English muffin and cream cheese when footsteps sounded moments before the knock at the door. "It's open."

The door inched open enough for Neil to pop his head in first, a frown on his face, followed by the door pushing fully open and him stepping inside. "Do you always invite people inside without asking who they are first?"

"Every single person." His eyes widened and she chuckled. "All three of you in as many years. You this morning. Becky when they ran out of sugar," squinting she glanced upward a minute calculating, "about a year ago, and the city inspector a while before that."

"I can't decide if you're kidding or not." His frown remained intact.

"About the three people? Not really. Living upstairs from a veterinary clinic, you don't get many unexpected visitors. Deliveries are all left at the clinic, so if someone knocks, like you just now, it's because I'm expecting them. And as I mentioned the other night, not a big dater. Besides, do they lock the doors at the ranch?"

"No, but that's different. Not many of the criminal element lurk out in the middle of nowhere looking for trouble."

"I suppose not, but the criminal element in Tuckers Bluff is usually limited to cow tipping and the occasional speeding ticket. I can't remember anything really dangerous happening around here since Meg was taken hostage at the feed store."

"What?" His head whipped around to look at her door.

"It's a long story. I'll fill you in on the drive."

Focusing on the door, he nodded. "Has anyone ever suggested a deadbolt for this thing?"

The widening protective streak in Neil towards her was enough to make a girl grin for a week. "I'm sure if DJ let Becky live here without a deadbolt, then it's perfectly safe for me too."

Lips pressed tightly together, he glanced one more time at the door before blowing out a long sigh, looking down at his watch and letting go of the frown. "We've got a lot of ground to cover and should probably get going."

Taking one last sip of her coffee, she nodded. "All set."

The first stop of the morning was a tile store on the very edge of Butler Springs. One display wall was prettier than the next. While Neil spoke with the sales person, she wandered around the different show areas.

"According to the salesman, everything with a red dot is in stock, blue dots are on sale, no dots means it has to be ordered and delivery time could be anywhere from one week to six months."

"Six months? For tile?"

He shrugged. "Could be coming on a slow boat from China or being handmade in Mexico. Lots of reasons for delays, but with the crew arriving in a few days, let's check out the red dots and if we like something in blue, even better."

They left the store with five different combinations that could work for the bathrooms and kitchen. En route to the next stop, she played with one pale blue rectangular tile. "I've always liked the look of subway tile. Even before it was popular."

"Some things are timeless. Like white appliances. They may not always be in vogue, but they don't date you either."

"That's for sure. Every time I visit my Aunt Hazel and walk into her kitchen and see the avocado green cooktop that just won't die, I'm reminded she hasn't remodeled that kitchen since 1968."

"The stove still works?"

She nodded. "And the oven too. Aunt Hazel says they were made before designed obsolescence became more important than pride in the product."

"Sadly, she's mostly right." He turned the corner and pulled into a massive parking lot in front of a building that looked to be in as bad shape as the homestead they planned to revive. "Let's see what we can find."

A broken ankle was the first thought that came to mind, followed by tetanus, but she opted instead to put on a smile and hope they found whatever he wanted fast. The moment she crossed the threshold she stood bathed in a flood of bright light from a twenty foot ceiling crammed with every size and shape chandelier imaginable. Any thoughts of falling through another rotted floorboard gave way to fascination and awe of all the magnificent pieces that filled the front room.

"I'm Neil Farraday. We spoke yesterday afternoon."

A slim man who looked to potentially be older than Moses shook Neil's proffered hand. "So you're part of the team rebuilding Sadieville?"

Neil nodded. "I am."

"Can't tell you how much I'm looking forward to seeing what you do with the place. I couldn't have been more than five or six when my granddad would take us for a Saturday drive to Sadieville for ice cream. Y'all redoing the old ice cream parlor?"

"The whole town."

The old man's face lit up. "Looking forward to seeing the town again for sure. Hope someone saved the ice cream recipe."

From chit chat about the old town the conversation progressed to what Neil was looking for and half an hour later she found herself in a partially open courtyard at Neil's side rummaging through section after section of old doors.

She had been tasked with helping to find a front door with a transom window above. When she reached the end of the row, she looked down the narrow walkway between the stacks of doors. "Good grief."

"What?" Neil stopped shuffling through doors and turned to her.

"There's more. At first I thought the doorway was just an emergency exit."

Neil nodded and came to stand beside her, blowing out a piercing whistle at the discovery. "I saw that. Passed it over as an exit."

"Pays to be snoopy." She lifted her chin and grinned at him.

Smiling, he nodded back. "An admirable quality."

"This place is like a bloody maze."

Standing in a section filled with every size mantle anyone could possibly want, Neil looked in her direction. "More doorways?"

"More like a lumberyard." She waved him over.

At her side, his jaw dropped and his eyes popped. "Holy oak wood." Before she could react, a huge grin on his face, he spun about and give her a bone crushing bear hug. "Pay dirt."

Left standing almost stunned in place, a small part of her wished she could find something else in this junkyard to make him so happy. She blinked and realized he was standing in front of one of many piles of old timber almost as tall as he was. "Are you planning on building a whole new house?" Why would anyone get so excited over piles of lumber?

A small piece of wood in his hand that he'd retrieved from one of the piles, his grin grew even wider. "Not a new house. An old floor."

She did a double take just as he turned the graying wood to expose a golden yellow grain with a faded shine. "That's a floor?"

"It all is. This is white oak. Enough to cover the old pine floors in half the town if we need it."

"And this is a good thing?" She didn't quite see why he

was so excited about an old floor. People installed new floors all the time.

"If you've ever picked up a two by four in the lumber store, you'd notice it doesn't weigh much. Then pick up an old two by four from a construction site where old wood has been torn out. The two by four is a lot heavier. A century ago old trees were felled to make lumber. Now, trees are grown specifically for lumber and cut down at a younger age. The rings aren't as tight and the wood not as dense. This," he waved the small piece in the air, "is a gold mine for restoration."

"Glad I could help."

"I would have walked right past that doorway. You're a salvage yard natural."

He walked away circling and reviewing all the piles, and she wondered if a salvage natural was anything like a junkyard dog, and if that was a good or bad thing?

Crumpling the wrappers from their burgers, Neil tossed them into the empty bag and swallowed the last sip of his cola before shifting the car into gear and pulling out of the lot. "We have one more stop." Never in all his years of sourcing products for his plans had Neil had so much fun. He loved rummaging through old salvage yards for period pieces that had been saved from demolition, especially when he found just the right items for a project. But beyond the shadow of a doubt, Nora was way better company than any of his brothers.

Monthly Garden Homes Magazine in her hands, Nora flipped a page and waved it at him. "This looks like the blue tile you picked. It's beautiful."

He nodded. "I've been thinking we might be able to make that work in the master bath."

"What about the other one?"

"I'm leaning towards more traditional. Something functional that looks period."

"I can understand that." Her head bobbed up and down as she closed the magazine. "So, where's the next stop?"

"A restoration shop."

"Restoration?"

"Yeah. That fellow at the salvage yard told me that a local restoration shop bought all their stand alone soaker tubs."

Her eyes rounded. "You mean like one of those claw foots?"

"That's what I'm thinking. If we can find one at a reasonable price that's already restored it will fit in with the schedule."

"It would be perfect."

"Exactly."

"There's one thing I don't understand."

"Shoot."

"I didn't think architects pick things out like tiles and light fixtures and things."

"Not many do." He turned the corner and pulled into the parking lot of the line of garage studios in the industrial side of town. "And personal things like paint colors and wallpaper and furnishings is usually on the client or their interior designer. When we started doing period restorations, we took over more of the responsibilities and developed a reputation for our work. We agreed in this project, because of the scope and tight schedule, that I would take the lead."

"From what I've seen so far, this is going to be great."

Parked, he hopped out and scooted around the car. "I've really appreciated your help."

"I didn't do anything really." Nora climbed out of the car and he almost grabbed hold of her hand. Instead he shoved his hands in his pockets.

"Don't underestimate your contribution. For starters, I would not have found those floors and they are going to look so much better than wider modern hardwoods."

"Can't you find hardwoods nowadays with the narrower planks?"

"Probably, but not without ordering it and—"

"There's no time for special orders."

They strolled into the building through an open garage door.

"I wouldn't have thought I'd say this, but this place makes the salvage yard look rather upscale."

He couldn't help laughing. "I have a feeling not many customers come here."

The shop did indeed have not one but several tubs.

"This is definitely the one." Nora looked up at him. "It's the perfect fit. Climb in and see."

Nora had climbed into every tub and leaned back. When she climbed into this one, her head went back, her eyes closed, and he assumed she was imagining herself submerged in a hot relaxing bubble bath. The problem was it took every ounce of will power he possessed not to do the same. "Thanks, but I think I'll take your word for it."

"Chicken." She extended her arm for him to grab her hand and help her out.

Just as he was about to gently tug her up, she gave a hard yank and sent him tumbling into the tub.

"See?" She chuckled. "Big enough for two."

He wasn't completely convinced. Especially since he could feel way too much of her, way too close. Doing his best not to flatten her under his weight, he scrambled up and out. "I think we'll put a hold on this one."

Sucking in a deep breath, there were a few more things he needed to put a hold on and none of them had anything to do with restoring a turn of the last century craftsman home.

CHAPTER SIX

Like half the population of the country, Nora loved watching all the fixer upper television shows. Whether filmed in the north, the south, during warm weather, cold weather, she loved them all. For years she'd kept a file of all the things she'd love to have in her perfect home. Some day. Though that some day was looking to be further and further away.

On the bright side, living in the apartment over Adam's veterinary clinic had been saving her a fortune, which meant her savings had been growing. She'd promised herself the day she graduated college, if she didn't already own her own home by her thirty-fifth birthday, then she'd buy one even if it meant buying it by herself.

"A penny for your thoughts." Neil glanced momentarily in her direction.

They'd left Butler Springs close to half an hour ago and had talked almost non-stop the whole time. Now, an easy silence had settled over them, and rather than feel the need to fill the quiet, her mind had wandered. "Not worth that much."

"Why don't you let me be the judge of that?"

"Buying my own home."

His gaze remained fixed on the road ahead and she realized as much as she'd learned about him on their recent drives, she knew he lived alone and not on the family ranch like some of his brothers, but she didn't have a clue if he owned or rented. Not that it mattered. "Sometimes I feel like the story of the shoemaker's children who went without shoes."

"Excuse me?"

"I fix houses for so many people, but not my own."

"So you own your own place?"

He shook his head. "I rent an apartment downtown. A loft, actually. Nice high ceilings. Few walls."

"I guess that makes decorating easier. Less vertical space to fill."

A small laugh bubbled to the surface. "I suppose there's always a silver lining. After all, a person can't be expected to hang pictures or paintings if there are no walls."

"See!" Those few words had her envisioning a typical bachelor pad. Big bulky leather furniture with clunky dark wood tables and nothing on the walls except for a massive television. "Do you cook?"

His gaze shifted from the barren and dusty roadway. "I can fend for myself in a kitchen."

Thoughts of an empty kitchen with two or three pots and pans at best and the same dishes from the college dorms completed her vision of his home.

"Do you cook?"

A grin pulled at her cheeks. "I can fend for myself in a kitchen."

This time he burst out laughing. "Touché."

Truth was, she was a pretty darn good cook. It just wasn't fun cooking for one most of the time. "If there's time before the film crew begins, maybe you can come by and I can make us dinner."

His smile bloomed wide and bright. "I'd like that."

"Do you have a favorite meal?"

"You mean meals. My mother would make enough dinner to feed half the town and as we scarfed it down she'd profess that the way to all of our hearts was definitely through our stomachs. But to answer your question, I loved Mom's stroganoff and lasagna. I used to think her pot roast was the best on the planet, but Aunt Eileen's cola roast beats it hands down. Just don't tell her I said that."

"Your secret's safe with me."

A loud bang, like a bullet firing, ricocheted in the cab of the truck at the same time the truck veered sharply to the left, then wobbled and teetered right. Neil spun the wheel, over corrected, and the vehicle tipped in the opposite direction. They were most definitely nearly out of control as Neil gave another quick tug at the steering wheel, and the truck teetered side to side long enough for Nora to say her prayers that the truck remained upright before they finally came to a stop. Her hands on the dashboard in front of her, she straightened in her seat, tugged the tightened seatbelt loose, and sucked in a long deep breath.

His hand reached out to touch her arm as his voice dropped low and deep. "Are you all right?"

The best she could do was nod. Apparently her nerves had regurgitated and were now stuck in her throat. When his fingers curled around her hand, she thought maybe having lost control of the car and scaring her half to death might have been worth it.

"Sounds like we blew a tire. I'm going to take a look."

Again, she nodded, then gulping down a calming breath, hopped out of the truck to stand by Neil at the rear of the truck. "This doesn't look good."

"It gets worse."

How a metal rim nearly to the ground with a large chunk of rubber stripped away from the very flat tire could get any worse, she didn't know. "How so? Or shouldn't I ask?"

"The spare is gone."

"Gone?"

He nodded. "It might have slipped my mind that after my last run-in with debris at a construction site and a flat tire, I didn't take the old tire in for a patch because it was pretty much time for new tires."

"So now what?" From what she could tell, they were halfway between Tuckers Bluff and Butler Springs, and AAA was less than predictable out in the middle of West Texas.

His phone already at his ear, he turned it away long enough to say, "Call in reinforcements." Another moment and pacing by the truck, he spoke into the phone. "Hey, Finn. I've got a situation here."

With Neil's back to her, Nora couldn't hear what Finn

was saying.

Neil gave his cousin the abbreviated version. "Great. Really appreciate it."

Keeping her eye on his phone as he slid it into his pocket, she waited for him to fill her in. A long moment passed. Patience was not one of her virtues. "What did he say?"

"He's going to come out to help, but first he has to procure a tire."

"And how long will that take?" She wasn't liking the direction this conversation, and rescue, was taking.

"No telling, but probably not long. Farradays tend to be resourceful. I'm sure he'll find something at the ranch that will work for us. A couple more hours and we should be home."

"I suppose, if a person had to be stranded somewhere, out here in the middle of nowhere with a blanket of stars overhead certainly beats some places I've been. Though I wouldn't mind a real blanket. It's starting to get chilly."

"Yeah." His gaze lifted upward. "By the time the sun fully sets it's going to be a lot more than just a little chilly."

There were a lot of things that made Neil unhappy. Blowing a tire in the middle of a West Texas highway surrounded by a lot of nothing was one of them. Not having a spare was another. Stranded and waiting with a fun, beautiful woman for his cousin to come to the rescue made up for both negatives on his list.

With the cold night air moving in, the best place to stay warm was inside the cabin of the truck. Hugging herself, Nora briskly brushed the sides of her arms, silently confirming his assessment. "Let's get back in the warm truck."

"You're probably right." Her gaze lifted heavenward. "How much longer do you think before the stars come out?"

Following her lead, he looked up and then across the

horizon and back. "Probably not before Finn gets here." At least he hoped not. One of the things you could count on this time of the year were sunny warm days and with the blink of an eye, cold nights would descend.

"Hmm." Her gaze drifted off into the distance. "I know we have plenty of stars in Tucker's Bluff, but I love the light show the sky puts on when there's a reason to be far enough from town."

He nodded. Anywhere with no light pollution always made stargazing something special. Once again she rubbed her arms and he was reminded of just how fast the temperatures could drop in this part of the country. "We'd better get in the truck."

"Just a few more minutes." She smiled at him and at that moment, if she'd asked him for the sun and moon, he would probably have tried for a way to give them to her.

Opening the door, he reached into the back seat and grabbed his jacket. "At least put this on." He slid the jacket over her shoulders.

Twinkling eyes met his. "Thank you."

They stood there a few more minutes, not saying anything, not really looking at anything, just taking in the grandeur of the simple world around them. "You know, I put in a lot of miles between here and Oklahoma. There are places just like this with a whole lot of nothing. No trees, no cows, horses, no houses, and certainly not any people. But I'm sorry to say, my mind is always on the next destination, the next set of plans. I really should take more time to stop and appreciate the world we live in."

Arms crossed, she leaned back against the truck. "There's a reason clichés live through generations. Stop and smell the roses applies to vegetation-limited West Texas. Though, stop and smell the fresh air would probably be more suitable."

"Stop and see the stars." He smiled at her, more pleased than he should be when she faced him and smiled back. Nora's weight shifted from one foot to the other and he realized just how long they've been standing, waiting. "Ready to sit inside yet?"

She shook her head.

If she wanted to be out in the fresh air watching the sunset—and depending on how long it took Finn, maybe even watching the stars—then he might as well make them as comfortable as possible. Anyone who drove as much as he did across barren country always kept a stash of emergency supplies. He had a couple of blankets in the back as well as water, flashlights, and other items to survive being stranded in inclement weather for long periods of time, and right now he wished a couple of pillows were considered emergency supplies.

"What's this?"

"Might as well get comfortable while we wait." He rearranged some of the items in the bed of the truck and folding the thicker blanket over a few times for padding, helped her onto the truck. "Not exactly five star accommodations, but the best I could do on short notice."

"Perfect."

"I've got extra if it gets too cold." He set the additional blanket beside her.

"Thanks." Her knees close to her chest, she wrapped her arms around her legs and tipped her head to face him. "When this remodel is a big hit, are y'all going to remodel the other homesteads?"

He shook his head. "I don't think so. We've got the hotel slated for the next project. The television producers, as well as the town council, want the ghost town renovations to move forward."

"It is a fun idea."

"It is. I don't know if it will be enough to convince the developers to put in the infrastructure for a residential neighborhood to go with a tourist town."

"It worked for Walt."

"Walt?"

"You know, Disney."

For the most part Neil considered himself a pretty smart guy, but he wasn't following her trend of thought at all.

Her eyes rolled skyward. "Besides the most popular amusement park in the world, he also envisioned the perfect home town. I forget the name of it, but people have been living there since the 90s."

"Of course. I don't think that we can compare Sadieville or West Texas to the most famous vacation spot in the world, but the idea of building a functioning town verses just a tourist attraction holds a lot of appeal."

"Really?" She continued to look at him.

"I always enjoy creating someone's vision, but I admit, hunting around today for this project in particular was especially fun." Even though he was pretty sure the company had as much to do with his good mood as the scope of the project.

"Some days I wish I were more creative." She turned her attention back to the almost set sun. "I don't really have any crafty skills. I can't knit or sew or paint or draw, but then I'm there when Brooks delivers a baby, or saves a person who goes into cardiac arrest, or even just working with nervous first time moms, or kids with colds, and I don't mind the lack of talent so much."

"The grass is always greener." He leaned back against the cab. "As a teenager I decided to take piano lessons."

"I'd love to be able to play the piano, but there's that lack of talent thing again."

"Yeah, well, so would I. Creativity with a pen and pencil does not translate to tickling the ivories. I finally had to give up. Though I do play a mean Heart and Soul."

"I guess it's human nature to want what we don't have."

He bobbed his head. "Most of the time you're probably right. If you could have anything at all, right this minute, what would it be?"

"You mean besides a medium rib eye with sautéed mushrooms and onions?" Her smile was infectious.

"Don't make me hungry. Yes, besides a steak."

Her eyes narrowed and she took so long to answer that for a few moments he thought she wasn't going to. "My own home."

"Brooks' old apartment isn't cutting it?"

"Yes and no. I love living there. I get to walk to work. My neighbors are peacefully quiet."

"No barking dogs?"

She shook her head. "Most overnight guests are recovering from some kind of treatment so they're not terribly vocal. Once in a blue moon they'll keep a dog that insists on making enough noise to be heard in New Jersey, but that's not the norm."

"Tell me about your dream home."

Immediately her eyes took on a renewed sparkle. "Nothing too big. Large enough for everyone to have space but small enough to feel cozy."

"Everyone?"

One shoulder lifted in a shrug. "I suppose a family, otherwise friends."

"Of course." Living alone in a big old rambling house didn't hold much appeal to him. Why would it appeal to her?

"There would be lots of light. I hate dark houses. That's one thing about the apartment I wish were different. There's only front windows in the living kitchen area so natural light is limited."

Note to self, lots of natural light. "What else do you want in your own home?"

"You don't want me to bore you with daydreams."

"I want to hear." He really did.

"I like marble countertops. I know they're more delicate, but they look nice. Remind me of my grandmother's kitchen. There was one spot on the counter that dipped from years of rolling out dough and baking."

"Nice memory."

"I think if she'd lived in this part of the state my mom would have kept the house. Anyhow, I want lots of closets. Which knocks the older, more affordable homes in Tuckers Bluff out of the running."

"You've looked."

Her nose crinkled in a cute grin. "I like snooping online. I figure if I know the market, when I'm ready to buy, I'll recognize a good deal."

"Smart. It's what we do. When Owen decides on a neighborhood worth investing in, he watches it for months and often recognizes a good deal before the competition."

"Y'all really like what you do."

He nodded. "Yeah. My uncle Phil on my mom's side once asked me what I wanted to do when I grew up. I answered I might want to be a lawyer. He then very seriously looked me in the eye and said, 'I didn't ask what you wanted to be, I asked what you wanted to do. Find something you love doing and you'll never work a day in your life.' I always remembered that. When it turned out that all the things my brothers and I liked doing somehow evolved around construction, well, the rest is history."

"I think I get it. I had a lot of fun helping Meg fix up the B&B with the family when she first bought it. Of course, it's especially fun when you're not spending your own money."

"There is that." He smiled. Ideas running through his head, he had an absurdly boyish need to hold her hand. Her hands at her side, resting on the blanket edge, long thin fingers were only inches away from his. It would be so easy to just slide his hand that short distance to close the gap and curl her hand into his. But there would be no one here to see them holding hands, no reason for the pretense. Here and now they were just friends. Barely friends. Only friends. So why was the word friends suddenly so distasteful?

CHAPTER SEVEN

"We need to check all the spares on the ranch trucks and cars. It's too easy to take for granted that nothing will happen on the road." Neil's Aunt Eileen set a hot pot of stew on the kitchen table.

"You know we check all the vehicles on a regular basis. And we do not leave the ranch without a functioning spare tire." Sean Farraday glanced briefly at his nephew. There was no need to say anything more. Neil got the message loud and clear.

Funny, but Neil knew his father was going to say the exact same thing to him the next time they spoke and in exactly the same tone. He also knew, now that his dad and his uncles were speaking to each other again, that whether or not he told his father about the incident, the next time he and his dad spoke, Patrick Faraday would know all about his son being stranded in the middle of West Texas without a spare tire.

"It was very nice of you to include us in dinner." Nora reached for a homemade roll. "I didn't realize how hungry I was until I got a whiff of your stew."

His aunt waved her hand in a dismissive gesture. "Y'all would have had to drive right past the ranch to get back to town and you know there's always plenty in this house."

The front door creaked open and quickly slammed shut. "Man, is that stew I smell?" DJ hung his hat in the front hall and nose to the air, made his way to the kitchen.

The family patriarch gestured for his son to take a seat. "If you're hungry, there's plenty."

"When it comes to Aunt Eileen's beef stew, I'm always

at least a little hungry."

Aunt Eileen pushed away from the table and turned to the cupboard for an extra place setting. "You still on duty?"

"Not officially." A deep line formed at the bridge of his nose. "There's a little issue that is spilling over into surrounding counties."

"How little?" Uncle Sean lifted his gaze from his dinner plate.

The way DJ's jaw twitched, Neil could tell whatever the issue was, it wasn't little at all. "I'll be stopping at the pub before I head home to give Jamie a heads up, might as well start here."

This time Finn froze, his fork halfway to his mouth. "The pub?"

"It appears Butler Springs has a date rapist on its hands."

"It appears?" Uncle Sean echoed.

The glare DJ shot his father caught Neil off guard. Never in his life could he remember his cousins being so blatantly disrespectful to their father.

"Recently, reports of date rape have been on the rise. At first the chief of police in Butler Springs didn't think the cases were connected, but the incidents continued to rise in frequency and a pattern began emerging. For starters," he looked from Nora to Joanna, "no more ladies nights at the Boot N Scoots. At least not for a while."

Eyes wide, both women nodded without saying a word.

"At first the incidents appeared isolated in connection with the Boots N Scoots."

"But not anymore?" Neil set his fork down, his appetite suddenly gone.

"As I said, the reports are on the rise and the locations where these women are being slipped a roofie are increasing as well."

Aunt Eileen shook her head. "I hate the thought that something so ugly is invading our little part of the world."

"And I'm doing my best to keep it out of Tuckers Bluff and Butler county, but the other night a woman in Poplar Creek was spared by an alert friend. She was dancing with someone when she noticed her friend at the table with a guy was moving funny. When she spotted the guy helping her friend stand and start walking toward the front door, she took off to catch up to them. The guy backpedaled immediately, claimed he was taking her outside for some fresh air and then offered to help the woman get her friend to the car. At first she didn't think anything of it, but her friend was out cold. Dead weight, by the time she was almost home, so instead she took her to the ER."

"She was drugged." His aunt's words were not a question.

DJ nodded. "Ketamine."

"Was the woman able to identify him?"

"They've got a sketch, but they'd both had a few drinks. The friend is pretty annoyed with herself for not having paid more attention, but…"

Everyone at the table understood. No one had law enforcement in the family and didn't learn that witness identifications were the least reliable source of information available. Getting two witnesses to agree completely on what they saw was about as common as winning the Powerball.

"So now what?" Neil asked.

DJ blew out a short sigh. "Law enforcement in three counties are doing their jobs and going to catch the SOB. Hopefully sooner than later. In the meantime, we need to keep our eyes and ears open."

Pictures of Nora alone at O'Fearadaigh's nursing a drink played in Neil's mind. The possibilities of some asshat coming along and taking advantage of her made him want to form an old-fashioned posse to find the guy and string him up like the animal he was. For just a minute, he thought of the ghost town. Maybe going back to a simpler time and place wasn't such a bad idea at all.

Dinnertime with the Farradays was one of Nora's favorite

things to do. Few families had the vibe that the Farradays did. No matter what was going on in their world, friends were always welcome, and anyone could count on the Farradays to have their back. It didn't hurt any that Aunt Eileen was a really good cook and Brooks had married a sensational baker.

What wasn't very exciting was the topic of conversation that had taken up most of dinner and was now continuing on the drive home. The idea that there was a serial rapist running around drugging women in bars made her want to throw up or lock herself in her apartment for the rest of her life. "I hope DJ and the other police chiefs catch this guy and soon."

"My money is on the good guys." A smile no doubt meant to reassure took over Neil's face.

Her money was on the good guys too. She knew here in town, at the pub, no one would be at risk. That annoying part of a small town that had every neighbor in everybody's business had a flip side. Because everybody was in your business, if you needed anything at all, somebody would be there for you. Especially if their last name was Farraday. As surely as she knew the sky was blue, she knew that nothing would happen to anyone under Jamie's watchful eye. She wouldn't be at all surprised to find a few extra Farradays hanging out on weekends just in case.

"Are you wearing your gun?"

Nora shook her head. "I usually keep it in the nightstand next to the bed. I really did only have it the other day in case of snakes."

"In a drawer is rarely close enough in a true emergency. Do you at least keep it loaded?"

"No card-carrying native Texan would be worth her salt if she didn't keep her gun loaded."

He nodded. "Would I be correct in assuming that this card-carrying native Texan can hit what she's aiming at?"

"That's a pretty safe bet." There were a few things in life—in her life—that were understood. She loved nursing, and was very good at it. Someday just like everybody else on the planet, her heart would stop. Taxes were always going to go up, and, at 30 feet she could shoot a man in the heart without so much as breaking a sweat.

"That makes me feel a little better. Not much, but a little."

"I know this thing that DJ brought up is unsettling." She didn't want to admit it had her downright spooked. "But as long as I don't try picking up any men at a bar or nightclub, I should be perfectly safe."

"Hmm."

She'd pay big bucks to know exactly what was going through that Farraday mind of his. They all had a chivalrous streak as wide as the Rio Grande. If that low life in Butler Springs knew what was good for him, he'd stay far away from Tuckers Bluff. "Do I need to remind you there have been no reports of trouble here in our town? Besides, you know we're all going to be watching out for each other until this nutcase is caught. It will probably be something very boring like a Son of Sam."

"Son of who?"

"Son of Sam. Did you ever watch true crime documentaries?"

"Nope."

"And there you go shattering my illusions of the typical male. I thought shoot 'em up, blood and gore movies were part of the male DNA."

"Well yeah, in a movie. But you're talking true crime."

"So you never watched a Bonnie and Clyde movie?"

"Of course I have. They were famous and from Texas."

"I rest my case. Shoot 'em up, blood and gore."

Neil laughed a low deep rumble and the sound made her toes tingle. "Okay, maybe a little, but no, I have no idea who the Son of Sam is."

"In New York, decades ago, he went on a killing spree murdering couples in parked cars. There was a massive manhunt for him. In the end they caught him because of a traffic stop. Rather anticlimactic. And I suspect that this creep will probably be found by something as equally innocuous."

"I don't care how they catch him, so long as they catch

him soon."

The town lights could be seen on the road ahead. Normally the drive from the neighboring ranches into town dragged on, but right now she wished it were even further away. "So, in the meantime, what happens now? With the show, I mean."

"Tomorrow I'm going to take my tires to Ned's and get replacements. Then I'm going to tweak some of the blueprints to better accommodate some of the pieces we found today, and then we get to present everything to the developers for a final approval. Then we can start the real work. And filming."

"When will the production people be arriving?"

"If all goes as expected, the whole crew will be here ready to shoot by Monday." Neil pulled into a parking spot in front of the clinic.

"I bet you're looking forward to getting started on this."

His hand on the door handle, he paused and looked at her. "Not at first. I truly wanted to throttle my brothers for agreeing to this mad dash of a remodel, but now," a smile took over his face, "yeah, I'm looking forward to this project more than I have to any other in a long time."

Before she could finish unstrapping her seatbelt, her car door swung open and Neil's extended hand waited for her. "Thanks." She knew there was no point in telling him he didn't have to walk her to her door. Chivalry rain deep in this part of the state, even if a man's last name wasn't Farraday.

Quietly, he followed her to the side door to the staircase up to her apartment. "Adam should have more light out here."

Keys in hand, she looked over her shoulder at Neil, then up to the small light that hung over the doorway. "It's all the light I need to find the keyhole."

A deep crease formed between his brows as he watched her turn the handle. Up the stairs, she slid the key into the knob and shoved the door open. "After tonight's conversation with DJ, I'm definitely talking to Adam about installing a deadbolt on this door and the one downstairs.

Any crafty kid with a plastic card and a bit of determination could let himself into both of these."

"I appreciate your concern, but I'm pretty sure except for Meg's crazy ex, no one has ever tried to break in. I figure as long as I stay away from swindling fiancés, I should be fine."

The crease remained between his brows. "Even in Tuckers Bluff a decent lock is a good idea."

She came within inches of arguing and just as quickly decided it was actually kind of nice to have someone worrying about her. "Thank you. Do you want to come in for a cup of coffee before the drive back?"

His gaze lingered over her shoulder. She wasn't sure if he was debating coming in, coffee, the drive back or something else. "Perhaps a rain check."

"It's a long drive back."

He nodded. "And I have an early morning. I think I'm going to crash over the café. Save myself an early morning drive back into town."

"Oh, that makes sense."

Once again, he glanced over her shoulder into her apartment for a long moment before letting his gaze settle on her. "I'd better go. Make sure to lock the door."

She nodded and smiled. "Always do."

"Okay, then." He sucked in a deep breath and took a step back. "I'd better go."

"You said that already." She had to fight the urge to step forward. Instead, she retreated half a step and for a split second thought she spotted disappointment in his eyes. She was crazy to think he was showing any more interest or concern than he would for any friend or even stranger. "Make sure to let me know how it goes tomorrow."

"Will do." Turning toward the steps, he placed his hat on his head and smiled at her. "Sleep well."

"You too." It took her a moment to realize he wasn't going to descend the stairs until she locked the door. Farraday or not, he really was something else. "Good night." She closed the door, turned the lock on the knob, and her hand still on the cold wooden surface, listened at the door until the last tap of his boot heel on the steps faded.

Stepping away, she pressed her lips tightly together, glanced at the living room window and told herself she would not spy on him crossing the street. She wouldn't. Then again, just because they were only pretending to date didn't mean that she couldn't keep a friendly eye out for a neighbor. She crossed the room and barely nudged the edge of her curtains in time to catch him stepping onto the curb across the street and disappear into the darkness she knew led to the café's rear stairs. And wasn't it a nice view.

CHAPTER EIGHT

DJ slid onto a stool at his cousin's pub. Even though O'Fearadaigh's was not open to the public for lunch, the family knew that any time they had a hankering for a corned beef sandwich, they were welcome.

"So what exactly is on your mind?" Jamie slid a dish with an open faced sandwich and a side of potato chips in front of his cousin.

"Same thing that's on every policeman's mind from here to Oklahoma."

Jamie bobbed his head and sighed. "Some days I wonder if the world has actually become so twisted, or if modern communications has made it impossible to live behind rose-colored glasses."

"Probably a little bit of both."

The pub door squeaked open, momentarily flooding the room with sunlight. His brother Adam removed his hat and took a seat beside his brother. "So, what is so all fired important that I had to actually take a lunch hour?"

"There was a break-in last night at Dr. Murphy's office in Poplar Creek."

Filling a glass with water, Jamie's head snapped up right. "Is the doc okay?"

DJ nodded. Dr. Murphy had a small veterinary practice in the next county. Nothing like Adam's operation, but big enough to attract the attention of the perp they were after. Like Tuckers Bluff, Poplar Creek was a growing community with a growing nightlife.

"I think I could use a glass of water." Adam spun around to face his brother. "Thieves or vandals?"

"Thieves."

"What did they get?"

"Ketamine."

Jamie set a glass of ice water in front of Adam, but addressed DJ. "What's that?"

Adam stole a chip from his brother's plate. "Most vets use it for anesthesia on cats."

DJ nodded. "It's also a popular date rape drug. Which means the clinic is going to need to take some extra precautions keeping your drugs under lock and key."

"Agreed." Adam nodded.

"You think this robbery is related to the incidents in Butler Springs?" Jamie poured himself a drink.

Right now DJ wished he weren't in uniform and could drink something stronger than water. He wasn't liking how this situation was spreading across counties too close to home. "If they're not, it's an awfully big coincidence."

"Who organized a party and didn't tell me?" The door squeaked shut behind Aunt Eileen.

"I really do need to oil those hinges." Jamie pressed his lips tightly together.

"Not often I see Adam's truck out and about town in the middle of the day." First glancing around the empty space, Aunt Eileen sat on DJ's free side. "I thought I might find some little ones here."

"Not today." Jamie got that same dopey grin he got whenever anyone talked about his wife or son. "Brendan's at Meg's. The cousins are all having a play date."

"So." His aunt's tone took on a more serious note. "Who wants to tell me what's going on?"

The door squeaked open again and all heads turned to watch Owen, Neil, and Paxton stroll through the door.

Raising a long cardboard tube in the air with one hand, Neil grinned at everyone. "Thought with all those cars out front we'd find some of y'all here. City Council and developers approved the drawings and the math. Looks like Sadieville is going to happen."

All three brothers slowed their steps, scanning the faces at the bar. Owen frowned. "Who died?"

"Sorry." DJ waved a hand at them. "Congratulations.

That will be a nice boon to the tax base. Which my department could use at the moment."

"Uh oh." Owen pulled a nearby stool over. "What's wrong?"

"This blasted date rapist is ticking me off."

"Another woman?" Neil's brows buckled, forming deep lines of concern.

"No." DJ shook his head. "But there probably will be soon."

Adam squeezed his eyes tightly shut before sighing and shaking his head. "Seems they've broken into a veterinary office to steal some drugs."

"The kind that will knock a woman off her feet in a not good way?" Owen said, his voice a little hoarse.

DJ nodded. "We need to catch this SOB and soon."

"What can we do?" Neil asked, the rest of the men at his side nodding.

"Keep an eye on the comings and goings of this town and this bar."

"That's easy." Aunt Eileen smiled. "We've got a bunch of old snoops who could put the CIA to shame. If some stranger comes sniffing around any of our women, he'll regret the day he was born."

Every person in the room dipped their chin in a unified nod of affirmation. DJ knew as well as the next guy that if any man were caught taking advantage of a woman—any woman, here or any place else—by the people he knew, all hell would break loose.

"Maybe I should hire a bouncer. Someone to make sure that every woman who comes in leaves on her own two feet."

"Do you get many strangers?" Paxton asked.

Jamie shrugged. "Not many. This is a family place in a small town, but the ghost town has brought us an uptick in tourists. It might be time."

"You know we'll all help?" Aunt Eileen fidgeted with a coaster. "We don't want to panic folks. Maybe just let a few more people know what we're concerned about."

"The word is out. It won't be long before news spreads

of the break-in. We can try to keep it on the low down, but…"

Everyone knew what DJ was saying, he didn't have to finish the sentence. And he knew he could count on all of his cousins to help, but they weren't law enforcement and this situation was a nasty mess. He hated every thing about it.

Neil pulled his truck into an empty space in front of Brooks' office. After Adam had returned to work, the rest of the family continued to discuss DJ's concerns with the recent burglaries and the implications. No place was perfect. Not even Tuckers Bluff. Still, even though the creep plaguing the county hadn't come anywhere near town, and hopefully wouldn't, the whole ugly situation hung over DJ and the town like a dark cloud.

Eventually the conversation shifted to the Council's approval of the homestead restoration and the mood of the room shifted. Once everyone headed home to the ranch, he begged off with some work he wanted to do on the schematics. What he really wanted was to take care of a promise.

"Well, isn't this is a nice surprise." A stack of files teetering in her arms, Nora came out from behind her desk.

"Here, let me help." He reached for the files.

"Thanks. We've been working on scanning all these old files into the new system. I guess I grabbed a few too many this trip."

"Where do you want them?"

With her chin, she pointed to the table along the wall behind the reception desk. "Scanner's over there."

He set the files to one side of the scanner, then turned in her direction. "The final drafts were approved today. I'm a little surprised how easy it was."

"I'm not. You're very good at what you do."

"And how do you know that?"

"You mean besides having seen your drawings and spending an afternoon with you fixture shopping?"

"That's certainly not enough to determine whether or not I'm any good at my job."

"No. But snooping in the portfolio shots on your website is. A few of the projects were simply jaw dropping. I mean," her cheeks singed a pale shade of pink, "not that they weren't all very good. They really were. It's just—"

He held one hand up and with his other hand placed a finger on her lips. "It's okay. I know what you mean. I don't love everything we do either."

She smiled. "So, what brings you here?"

"A celebration. I hoped you would join me for dinner at the pub."

"Oh." Surprise took over her face. What he couldn't determine was if it was a pleasant surprise, or a *how do I politely get out of this mess* surprise.

"The plan was to go out a few times before you dump me." He flashed a weak smile. "But if you have other plans…" he let his words hang.

"No. My only plans tonight involved a frozen dinner and streaming an as yet to be determined movie."

"Good. I'll pick you up at six?"

A smile bloomed wide on her face. "I'll be ready."

An unexpected surge of contentment overrode his earlier sense of disappointment that his invitation might have been distressing to her. Under the circumstances, feeling happy over a fake date probably wasn't a very good thing.

The way a swarm of butterflies fluttered madly in her stomach, anyone would think that she had been invited to Cinderella's ball by a crown prince. There was nothing about a quick dinner at Jamie's pub that justified how excited she was. All the more reason why she should have made more of an effort to date all these years. A simple dinner with a nice guy—a *fake date* with a nice guy—and she was fluttering about as nervously as the butterflies in her stomach.

Three dresses sprawled on her bed and she needed to make up her mind fast what to wear. She had spent nearly half an hour debating whether to just throw on jeans and boots like everybody else, or treat this like a date and wear a dress. Once she'd settled on the latter, she narrowed her choices down to three casual dresses. Neil would be here to pick her up any minute and greeting him in her underwear was not recommended. Unable to make up her mind, she finally settled for eenie meenie minie mo. The dark blue knit dress won. And in the knick of time. She'd slid into a pair of slingback sandals when she heard footsteps bounding up the stairs.

As a soft rap on the door sounded, she brushed her hands down her sides, smoothing non-existent wrinkles and taking in a deep breath, flung the door open. The sight of Neil Farraday standing with a bouquet of flowers in hand almost stole her breath.

"These are for you." He extended his arm and rocked back on his heels. "There's a new flower shop in town. I thought I'd give them a little boost in business."

"They're lovely. Thank you." There wasn't a girl alive who could resist taking a whiff of the beautiful blooms. And these were wonderful. "Come in. Give me a minute to put them in water."

"There's a small packet of something to sprinkle in the water attached to the ribbon. The gal in the store said they should last at least a week that way."

"Got it." Nora hurried across the room to the kitchen sink. It had been ages since anyone had given her flowers. The gesture had her grinning like the Cheshire Cat. She couldn't help herself.

Neil followed her into the kitchen. "I ran into Adam today at the pub during lunch."

"Oh, that's a surprise. Adam and Brooks are cut from the same cloth. Neither one of them usually leaves the office for lunch. If they eat at all it's at their desk or taking a few bites running down the hall from one room to another."

"DJ wanted to talk to him and I just happened to stop in."

"DJ?"

"Yeah. This date rapist thing has really gotten under his skin."

Even though she barely knew Neil, she could still tell there was something he wasn't telling her. "What aren't you saying?"

Quickly he explained about the veterinary clinic break-ins and the connection with the case in Butler Springs. "I spoke with Adam and we agreed that now would be a good time to install deadbolts on your doors."

Normally she felt perfectly safe here with just the locks on the doorknobs, but after hearing all the stories, she had to admit to herself she was a tad nervous. Still, she wasn't convinced turning her home into Fort Knox was the answer.

"Up to you? Now or after dinner?" he pressed.

"I don't suppose tomorrow is an option?"

He shook his head. "It's today or I sleep on your sofa."

The lazy grin that teased one side of his mouth had her biting back a grin of her own. "Oh, wouldn't that get the gossip mill going. How long will it take?"

"About fifteen minutes. Won't take but a minute or two to drill the holes then install the lock."

"Let's get her done."

True to his word. Thirty minutes later she had two new locks on her door, beautiful flowers in her kitchen, and was strolling into O'Fearadaigh's on the arm of a Farraday. For the first time in her life she was probably the envy of every single woman in town.

Just to add to the gossip mill, Neil requested a table in the far corner. The location was ideal for folks who wanted privacy, or in their case, who wanted to make a point. Their table was close enough to the dance floor if they wanted to partake, and far enough away that they didn't have to battle the music to hear each other. As far as she was concerned, they had the best seat in the house.

"My cousin was a genius for opening this place here in

Tuckers Bluff."

"Not to mention that he made all of our lives so much easier. If anyone wanted to celebrate a special occasion we'd have to drive out to Butler Springs. Not that Abbie's isn't a nice dinner, but the café is just not, you know, the ideal date night."

"Better not let Abbie hear you saying that."

"Are you kidding? She says that herself."

"She is a sharp lady."

"Sharp, and nice." Nora took a sip of her wine and caught a glimpse of Burt Larson from the hardware store and the bona fide town gossip, sitting near the bar. "Don't look now, but we seem to have drawn a few people's attention."

"Well, that was the idea." He pushed to his feet and extended his hand. "Shall we really give them something to talk about?"

She chuckled at his choice of words. "I'd be delighted."

A soft tune she didn't recognize played overhead as she curled into his arms and began a simple two step around the small patch of dance floor.

"I don't know who picks the music, but they have great taste."

With a short nod, she mumbled her agreement but didn't want to stop swirling to the music. Truth was that she probably wouldn't have much longer with Neil and at least for a little while tonight, wanted to pretend that all was well in the world, and maybe all between them was just a little bit real.

CHAPTER NINE

Only two days had gone by since dinner with Nora, and Neil was itching for an excuse to see her again.

"How is everything coming together?" Aunt Eileen set a plate of bacon down in front of him.

"Great." Owen stabbed at a pancake. "We're meeting the film crew out at the site today."

Aunt Eileen took a seat beside her nephews. "Oh, I didn't realize filming was starting already."

"It's not." Neil shook his head. "It's a pre-shoot checklist. Apparently they map out the placements and cameras and set up some of the spontaneous scenes."

"Isn't set up and spontaneous a bit contradictory?" Uncle Sean asked.

"Apparently," Neil met his uncle's gaze, "reality is a misnomer. Quite a bit is almost scripted. Hopefully we won't be too boring for them or it will be more scripted than less."

"I see."

"Ideally," Neil faced his aunt, "we'll be ready to roll on Monday."

By the time the family had finished their morning meal and headed out to do ranch work, and his brothers had finished laying out the plans for the shooting to his aunt and uncle, the sun was burning bright and Neil was ready to get moving. He had a call to make on his way and he wanted to get to it.

His truck kicking up dust on the way to the main road, Neil tapped his phone and waited for the sound of a now familiar voice.

"Hello," the scruffy sound was not what he expected.

According to the dashboard clock it was a quarter after nine, not too early to call. Was it? "Did I wake you?"

"No. Just a morning frog in my throat. Waiting for the coffee to finish brewing."

Crud. It hadn't occurred to him that people who aren't ranchers or construction workers wouldn't be up with the chickens. "I'm sorry."

"Don't be. I've been awake for over an hour but didn't feel like dragging myself out of the warm bed until a few minutes ago."

A vision of her tangled in sheets and blankets rubbing sleep from her eyes popped into his head. A mind picture he most definitely did not need to dwell on.

"You didn't call to see if I was still sleeping, did you?"

Redirecting his thoughts to today's plans, he actually shook his head and refocused. "No, I am heading out to the homestead to meet some of the production crew. Then we're going to walk the town to determine this season's shooting schedule. I'm not sure if your interest in rehab shows extends to seeing them behind the scenes, but since we should be seen together anyhow, I wondered if you might be interested in—"

"Yes!" she cut him off. "I can be dressed in ten minutes. How far away are you?" She waited a fraction of a beat. "Or do you want me to meet you out there?" Before he could form another word, she rambled on. "Or did I jump the gun? Was that not an invitation?" She sighed heavily. "I really should wait till after my morning coffee to speak."

"Yes," he chuckled. "That was an invitation. And yes, I thought I'd pick you up since I have to go through town to pick up some paperwork from the office. I meant to bring it home last night, but—"

"You forgot," she finished his sentence for him.

Of course she had no idea that he forgot because his mind was on their dinner the other night and debating if asking her to join him again would have been too much. In the end, he talked himself out of calling her and was halfway to the ranch before he remembered he hadn't grabbed the plans he needed. "I had a lot on my mind."

"I bet. This project is not a small undertaking."

"I'll be there in about thirty minutes."

"Have you eaten yet?"

The family had been up before the sun and before the first light of day had consumed a ranchers breakfast that would hold them steady for a hard days work. He'd eaten more than his fair share. "Have you ever been at the Farradays for breakfast?"

A burst of laughter erupted through the phone line. "Only once. Dumb question. I'll be ready when you get here."

The call disconnected and he pulled onto the main road, a smile on his face, looking forward to whatever the day had ahead. But first he had another stop he wanted to make.

The doorbell rang and Nora's head snapped up. Nobody ever rings her bell. Apprehension gripped her, and a tinge of panic trickled up her spine until common sense shouted at her that bad guys do not ring doorbells. "You really have to get a grip on your nerves."

No point in running back and forth. She grabbed her purse and trotting down the steps, midway to the ground floor, through the small glass pane, she could see a snapshot view of the brim of a tan hat. A few more steps and big blue eyes connected with hers, confirming her assumptions. Neil. It only took another second or two to remember she was now the proud resident of a doubly locked apartment. Every visitor would require her running downstairs to unlock the door. She'd have to look into some kind of smart lock, something she could unlatch from the comfort of her sofa and her phone.

"All set?" Neil grinned at her from the other side of the threshold.

"All set." Outside, she pulled the door closed and locked the deadbolt. "I'm really glad you thought to let me tag along. I can't resist that old town."

"I'm glad for the company. I love my brothers, but when they get on a bandwagon of some kind or other, heaven help anyone who disagrees."

"Are you expecting to disagree?"

He chuckled and held the car door open for her. "We wouldn't be brothers if we didn't."

"But this is business."

"And blood is thicker than water. Doesn't matter." He waved a finger at the box on the console between them. "I picked something up. Just in case you're a little hungry."

She recognized the box from the café. One little peek and the delicious aroma of fresh baked croissants tickled her nostrils.

"I wasn't sure if you preferred salty or sweet, so I got both. The croissants because I'm told Toni's are better than Paris bought, and the cake balls as well as mini blueberry muffins."

"Blueberry muffins?" She pinched a small morsel and tossed a bite into her mouth. The urge to groan with delight was almost too much to stifle. "I love everything Toni bakes, but I had no idea she was doing blueberry muffins now. I love blueberry."

"Me too. She had cranberry muffins also, but the blueberry called my name."

She popped the last piece into her mouth and then licked her fingers. "I can't tell you how glad I am you picked blueberry. These are amazing. Which, of course, is no surprise. Do you want one?"

"Thanks, but I actually downed a couple while waiting for Abbie to box up the rest of the order."

"Smart man."

"Remember to tell that to my brothers when I say one thing and they say another."

"Deal."

By the time they reached the old homestead, she'd eaten another mini muffin as well as two croissants. The cake balls could wait for the ride home.

"Looks like just about everyone is here." Several cars and trucks were parked in front of the old house and even more people were already mulling about. Neil grabbed his designs from the seat behind him and ran around the hood.

Nora slammed her door shut just as he reached her side of the car. "Did I mention how exciting this is? To see first hand how these shows are done?"

He shook his head. "Let's hope we don't bore that excitement into the ground by the time we're done."

Someone had set up a long folding table in the kitchen. The heart of the house. Nora stood to one side watching and listening as the siblings pointed at the papers, then at the ceiling and walls, and back to the papers. Neil made a few notes while the film crew measured what she assumed was light levels and hauled in equipment. She hadn't noticed the last time they were here, but the ceilings were higher than the standard eight feet giving the space a larger feel. Too bad somewhere along the way the average ceiling height had dropped. Though modern construction seemed to be doing their darndest to make up for it. So many designs not only had the taller nine or ten foot ceilings, but the two story living rooms that probably cost a fortune to heat or cool in the often extreme Texas weather.

"Come on," Neil ran his finger across the flat page, "we've done this before. It will look great."

Ryan pressed his lips together and stared down at the paper. "Of course we know it will be perfect, but it's outside the scope of the original conditions."

"And the city council approved them no problem."

"Yes." Owen raked his fingers through his hair. "But I promised the investors that we could deliver what they wanted within budget and bumping this out is not in the budget. Original square footage was the deal."

Nora couldn't resist inching closer to see what they were debating, until she was standing beside Neil and staring at the blueprints that might as well have been a Picasso painting for all the sense they made to her. "What is the debate about?"

"This." Neil lifted the first page, exposing the page underneath, and pointed. "An attached garage with a real laundry room."

"The original design is real." Ryan glared at his brother.

"He has a point." Owen sighed. "Butt bumper laundries get the most complaints."

"Butt bumper?" Nora asked.

Neil chuckled. "It's when the washer and dryer are placed in a pass through hall from the garage to another room like the kitchen or family room. Anyone standing in front of the machines doing laundry gets their butt bumped by a door if another person is coming in or out of the neighboring room."

"Oh yeah." Nora nodded. "Shannon complains about not having any place for her ironing board or the litter box."

"Litter box?" the brothers echoed.

Nora shrugged. "Laundry rooms are all purpose for most women. Extra fridge, or freezer, ironing space. A sink is always a nice touch, but even nicer is a place for delicates air drying to drip."

When she lifted her eyes from the papers, Neil stood with his arms crossed grinning triumphantly at his brothers.

Ryan was the first to sigh and nod. "I guess we're adding a real laundry room."

"And I," Owen sighed, "get to figure out how to pay for it."

At that moment Paxton popped out of a cut out in the hall and jumped to the ground. "If you're going to put an attached garage, why don't we add a real staircase?"

"What?" Owen's eyes widened into perfect circles. "Are you trying to bankrupt the project or kill our reputation, or both?"

"I know the cost of wood has gone up, but we're not talking about a major expense." Paxton brushed his hands together. "That attic is high enough for a second floor."

"Oh, just shoot me now." Owen dropped his forehead into his hands and shook his head. "You're killing me."

"I'm not saying add a second floor. I'm saying there's room up there if someone wants to expand some day and putting in a staircase would make more sense and not be much more expensive than a pull down ladder."

"What about a closet door?" Nora asked.

The four brothers turned to face her.

"Excuse me?" Neil asked.

"You know. Like up north." The blank stares told her they didn't have a clue what she was talking about. "Up north, most older homes that have full attics have a closet door on the second floor that isn't a closet at all, it's a staircase."

Neil bobbed his head. "Dutch colonials, Cape Cods and the like, the standard blueprints allow for a hallway staircase. It could be done. Here." He pointed to a spot on another page.

Owen stared at his brother's finger. "And how much more money are we talking?"

"Some two by fours, sheetrock, a door, and treads," Ryan said. "We don't have to do finished oak for attic steps. Sanded pine will work. Honestly, even with recent price hikes, I don't think we're talking more than a few hundred over budget."

"If it's more," Owen stared Ryan down, "it's coming out of your salary."

This time Ryan laughed and Nora had the feeling that this little clash of opinions was neither the first nor last time that the brothers had sparred, and was exactly what Neil had expected.

Back slapping and hand shaking took place, and while Owen took a few minutes to chat with the production crew, Neil sidled up beside her and leaning closer, whispered in her ear. "Thanks."

"For what?"

"For reminding my brothers I'm a smart man."

She couldn't help but smile. As a matter of fact, pretty much everything he said made her want to grin like the village idiot. And what the heck was she supposed to do about that?

CHAPTER TEN

"Why does the sermon always run long on the Sundays when we've got company coming for supper?" Eileen looked at her watch for the umpteenth time since pulling out of the parking lot at church.

"How many people are we expecting?" Sean Farraday climbed out of the truck and met his wife at the passenger door. "It's not like we don't have a full house on any given Sunday."

"Valerie has the production crew joining us."

That caught Sean's attention. "How many is that?"

"Valerie thought there might be four or five extra for supper. Some of the crew aren't needed right away. And I think the editors stay in LA."

Car doors slammed behind them as more cars made their way down the drive.

"I brought the bread." Toni carried a shopping bag in each hand and smiling, held her arms up at Aunt Eileen. "Can't have pasta without my Boston recipe for Italian bread. My mom bartered it out of a baker in Little Italy."

Eileen reached for one of the bags. "What did she have to barter for that little coup?"

"She says her soul, but I think it was her grandmother's recipe for Swedish meatballs."

"I didn't know your great grandmother was Swedish."

Toni laughed. "That's because she wasn't, but when they first came to Boston she worked as a cleaning lady. Mostly nights, for one of the bigger hospitals. She and the other cleaning ladies exchanged recipes. The Swedish meatballs were always a favorite."

"Hey, beautiful." Carrying their daughter Helen on his shoulders, Brooks sidled up beside his wife. "How lucky can a guy get, walking home with three beautiful ladies."

Helen giggled and Toni smiled up at her husband. More car doors opened and closed. One by one little children climbed out from their parents' cars. Some toddling better than others, but all laughing and giggling and running around. Eileen couldn't think of a prettier sight.

Neil's truck pulled up and he and Nora climbed out.

"What do you know about those two?" Toni kept her gaze on the couple strolling in their direction.

Eileen watched the happy body language of her nephew and long time poker playing friend. "Hard to say. Though I think they've passed smitten and are working toward solid." What she wasn't saying was that she'd feel a whole lot better about the relationship if there was a gray dog circling around them.

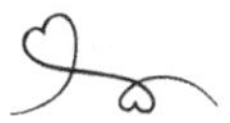

"You ever get the feeling every pair of eyes is on you?" Nora was getting used to it. There was something deep down inside her that wanted to do a jig when she considered that this time the gossip mill was focused on what a coup for her snagging a Farraday instead of how she was always lucky in cards and unlucky in love.

"Lately, more often than not."

At least he didn't seem upset by the attention they had garnered. That was the upside. The downside was that pretty soon she was gonna have to put an end to this ego boosting charade.

"Hold up." The only one dressed in a skirt with high heels, Morgan's wife Valerie came hurrying behind them.

Neil slid his hand around the small of Nora's back to bring her to a stop. Another flutter of delight struck her when he left his hand.

At their side now, lifting large dark sun shades onto her head, exposing twinkling eyes, Valerie looked to Neil. "One of my camera crew was telling me that you guys had a little disagreement about how to proceed with the decor."

"It wasn't really a disagreement."

"Mark got some of it on film. Fantastic material. We might need to reshoot some of it. I know Sunday suppers are all about family, but it wouldn't be a bad idea to go over some of the scripts."

"Scripts?" Nora asked.

Valerie shrugged. "We have to keep things interesting."

Eyes narrowed, a deep crease formed between Neil's brows. "There wasn't any scripting when we filmed the Mercantile episode."

"That's right. But last time, we had a ghost. The fact that they turned out to be crooks just made the ghost angle all the more interesting."

"Are y'all going to stand there blocking traffic all day?" Morgan stopped at his wife's side and keeping his hands on his crutches, gave her a gentle kiss on her temple. "I understand Aunt Eileen has had spaghetti sauce simmering all day using Toni's mother's recipe."

"I thought her regular sauce was pretty good." Nora had eaten with the Farradays enough times through the years to have tasted at least once everything Eileen made, and none of it was ever anything less than delicious.

"I'm sure whatever recipe she uses, supper's going to be wonderful." Unable to loop his arm around his wife the way he might normally have, Morgan gave her a wink. "We'd better get inside."

As more of the family and crew arrived, conversations ran in every direction. Somehow, between bites and raves over the new recipe, the discussion kept circling back to how much of the new show needed scripting.

"This isn't daytime television." Morgan reached for another slice of bread.

"True," Meg agreed. "I don't watch the home improvement shows for infighting."

"As a matter of fact." Catherine looked to Valerie. "Too often I wish they'd just let the shows do their thing instead of making a big fuss over some little thing as though it's the end of the world. We know darn well anything can be fixed and there's always a way to borrow from Peter to pay Paul. On top of that, when they give one of the homeowners an obnoxious personality all it does is makes me want to flip channels."

"Agreed." DJ's wife Becky nodded. "There's one couple in particular where the woman always spends too much on what she wants, and never gives the homeowner the one thing they really wanted. Every show you know what's going to happen. It's worse than a predictable novel."

"Oh-kay." Valerie's brows lifted high on her forehead. "Duly noted. Not that the brass agrees with you, but I'll keep it in mind. Who knows, maybe another ghost will show up."

A few people laughed, a few more rolled their eyes, and Aunt Eileen shook her head. "I don't know if we can handle any more ghosts. Fake or otherwise."

"Here here." Ted, one of the cameramen who filmed the pilot, nodded. "I can do without anymore footstools going bump in the night."

"I can't believe I forgot about all that." Nora hadn't been there at the time, but for days of filming, the ghosts were all the town could talk about. When the culprits turned out to be nothing more than a bumbling stolen dog ring, the truth had been rather disappointing to a lot of folks who were hoping to have a real life ghost town.

"I'll never forget." Valerie rubbed her hand against her throat reminding Nora that Morgan's wife had been snatched by the thieves. "But it does prove the old adage that most criminals are seriously stupid."

Again people laughed, except DJ. All afternoon he'd seemed distracted. A few times Nora had noticed him checking his phone or his watch and wondered if that blasted creep drugging women was what had him looking so serious.

"Something wrong?" Neil leaned into her. "You have that worried look on your face."

"I have a worried look?" Pulling her gaze away from

DJ, her eyes leveled with Neil's. A softness laced with concern focused on her.

"Maybe worried was the wrong word. Unpleasantly thoughtful. You had the same look on your face when we walked into the back of the salvage yard. And, well, that first night at the pub."

"I freely admit at the salvage yard I was wondering what the heck had I gotten myself into."

"Honestly, at first you looked as if I'd walked you into a pit of rattlers."

"Yeah, well." She laughed. "It felt that way. Especially when we started moving all those dusty doors. I kept thinking something was going to jump out and bite me."

"So what's going to bite you now?"

"Nothing. I was thinking about DJ. He looks awfully serious, which I guess in turn has me wondering if we shouldn't all be a little concerned." Of course she was probably overreacting. Criminal things happened all the time in the county that she most likely never knew anything about. As a matter of fact, DJ had that same look on his face when they'd first figured out Jake Thomas was no longer the sweet kid they'd grown up with but an abuser.

"I'm sure whatever is on his mind, he'll take care of."

"I'm sure he will." She glanced at all the people in the room, the couples who looked so happy together, the friends teasing and making jokes, and then she looked at Neil already in conversation with his brother at his other side. He really was a nice guy, but unlike the others, his interest in her was only make believe.

Apparently her lack of luck in love was holding. Finally, a great guy falls into her world who can almost read her mind and it was nothing more than a friendly game of pretend.

"It's interesting how places can geographically not be that far apart, and yet feel as far away as the sun from the moon." At the back porch railing, Neil wouldn't mind grabbing a bed roll and sleeping out in the pasture under the stars.

At his side, his brother Owen leaned over the same rail. "As a kid I remember loving the stars out here. Always wondered how we wound up so far away and so close to the city."

A beer in hand, Adam pushed at the floor and sent his rocker swaying. "Did either of you have any idea what caused the rift in the family?"

Neil turned to face his cousins sitting in matching dark green rockers. "Always wondered what went wrong. Mom had made it sound like we weren't welcome here anymore."

"I remember Uncle Brian telling us how lucky he was that his wife appreciated the ties of the Farraday clan." Finn took a sip of his beer. "I can't imagine what I would do if Joanna decided she wanted to leave here and move to another state."

"Ditto." Adam tipped the longneck in his brother's direction. "Are we sure Aunt Mariah was the reason and not Uncle Pat?"

Finn shrugged. "Dad said that when he and Uncle Pat finally talked over helping Chloe out, he got the idea Uncle Pat had been a reluctant participant in the separation."

The screen door swung open and DJ joined the men.

"You look like someone ran over your puppy." Owen straightened and crossed his ankles. "Anything we need to know about?"

DJ blew out a long sigh and ran his hand behind his neck. "Another report came in from Spring Rock. Same scenario. Tox panel shows Ketamine in the victim's blood."

"Blast." Finn leaned forward. "Any leads on the guy doing this?"

DJ shook his head. "The thing that bothers me is for every woman who comes forward, we know there are more who won't. This is a bigger mess than it looks like. I can feel it in my bones." He turned to Adam. "I need you to check your drug supplies. We've put out word to every vet within a hundred mile radius. Turns out that at least two offices have a shortage of Ketamine. They hadn't even realized they'd been broken into."

"How can you not notice your place of business has been breeched?" Neil didn't get it. Surely there would have been some clue.

DJ shrugged. "Cheap old locks. Unlocked windows."

"Makes me especially glad I put new locks on Nora's doors." Neil glanced toward the house and the women inside.

"Thanks for that. It never seemed that important before." Adam pulled out his phone and tapped the screen. "We're monitoring a Great Dane for a possible twisted intestine. I've got a tech there keeping an eye on him overnight."

Everyone kept their gazes on Adam as he explained to the tech what he wanted to know. Then they all waited silently while the tech checked the supplies against the inventory.

"Thanks, Jed." Adam ended the call. "Nothing's missing."

"I don't know whether to be relieved that you weren't targeted," Finn leaned back in the rocker, "or concerned that now you *could be* a target."

The same thought crossed Neil's mind. If this guy was out for more knockout juice, there were no guarantees that Adam's clinic wouldn't be on the guy's shopping list sooner than later. And there was no missing that Nora lived too close for comfort. That discomfort left him with two choices. Sleeping on the sofa of her place, which would really send rumors flying, or sleeping at the office and watching her place like a hawk with a mouse in his sights. "Is there an alarm system at the clinic?"

"No. Not the apartment upstairs either."

His cousin knew what he was thinking without him having to come right out and say it.

"I'll take care of that tomorrow. First thing," Adam reassured him.

He had the distinct feeling that putting in an alarm system was going to be much better received than him sleeping on the sofa. Too bad, he'd have felt better knowing he and Smith and Wesson would be on the job.

CHAPTER ELEVEN

"It's bad enough I now have to run up and down the stairs to let friends in, I really don't need an alarm system on top of that." Nora stood over the kitchen sink, a finger in one ear, the phone at her other ear, and her gaze fixed on the slowly brewing coffee pot.

The buzzing sound of the technician's drills poking through a new spot in the ceiling made it hard to think. She had presented her case against an alarm system more than once since Adam had told her about his plans at supper last night. What she hadn't expected was for Adam to have saved the owner of the alarm company's golden retriever after the pup had been hit by a car. Instead of having time to talk Adam out of the plan, the grateful alarm guy bumped Adam's install request to the top of the schedule.

"Everyone agrees this is important." Brooks was obviously not going to be any help in convincing the Farradays that she was perfectly safe without all the extra precautions. "Don't worry about coming in today. Toni will love an excuse to come help as soon as she drops Helen off at her play date. Make sure they get the job done right."

Like she would have any idea if these people were installing an alarm or a stereo system. Her call ended, she took a minute to run downstairs. Maybe there was a little more peace and quiet at the clinic—and already brewed coffee.

On the phone, Ian's wife Kelly looked up from her desk and held one finger at Nora. "Yes, Mrs. Peabody. Thank you for understanding." Kelly nodded at the phone a few more times, repeating, yes, ma'am, and finally disconnected the call.

The whirring of drills echoed through the clinic. “I see it’s not any quieter down here.”

“Nope.” Kelly blew out a sigh. “I can’t even hear myself think.”

“I tried to tell your boss, and anyone who would listen, that I didn’t need a new alarm system.”

“You may not,” coming out of his office, Adam pointed to a wire dangling from a newly made hole in the hallway, “but it’s high time that the clinic got an updated alarm system. Technology has changed dramatically in the last decade and we’re still functioning with locks and keys.”

Kelly shrugged apologetically at Nora before turning to her boss. “I’ve moved several appointments around and am waiting to hear back from a few more.” Kelly brushed some sheet rock dust off her desk. The more holes these guys drilled for wires and sensors, the more dust that built up. “Maybe we should just put up a gone fishing sign.”

“That’s actually not a bad idea.” Adam looked in the direction the whirring drill bit sounds seemed to come from. “Let’s get on the phone, tell everyone that we’re closed for the day and anyone who can’t wait to see me, I’ll do a house call.”

“Works for me.” Grinning, Kelly lifted her hand and gave Adam a thumbs up, then sat down and picked up the phone again.

Adam turned to face Nora. “I really am sorry about the noise and mess, but this needed to get done and now was as good a time as any. If you can talk my brother into giving you the rest of the day off, you should go shopping or out to lunch with a friend, my treat.”

“I just might do that.” Dueling drills were wearing down her last nerve. Not that he needed to treat her to anything, but instead of the town feeding the crew, the production company had brought in a food truck. And not a greasy spoon truck either, but one of those specialized ones that made your mouth drool. Driving over to check out the new truck for lunch was the perfect excuse for a little visit to one architect turned carpenter.

Back in her apartment she poured a hot cup of coffee,

changed out of her uniform into jeans and her favorite boots, and waited for the sound of guys scurrying in her attic like hyperactive squirrels to come to a stop. One quick tutorial later on how to work the system that actually included not only a camera view of the front doors, both the main door and at the top of the stairs, they'd blessedly installed a smart app to unlock the door from her apartment. Maybe letting the men have fun with their new toys wasn't such a bad idea after all.

Thrilled to have a good excuse to head out to the film site, she bounced down the stairs and out the door. Blasting her radio to volumes worthy of a live band performance, she sang all the way to the ghost town and beyond to the homestead. The activity buzzing about was more than she'd expected to find. Slowing as she approached, she fought back second thoughts and pulled her car up next to a pick up truck in a makeshift parking area.

Bumping her door shut with her hip, she marched across the dusty land and considered how to approach without interrupting.

"Nora!" Darting across the lot of vehicles, Valerie waved at her. Nobody else in town dressed up jeans, boots, and a cowboy hat the way she did. Always wearing dark, interesting sunglasses, an air of sophistication followed her no matter the wardrobe.

"Hope I'm not coming at a bad time."

"Not at all. I can use a change of pace." Val looped an arm with Nora and led her across the remainder of the lot, weaving through trucks and equipment before finding Neil wielding a circular saw on the front porch.

If Nora had thought the guys drilling holes and running wires at her place this morning were noisy, all the sawing and compressors and nail guns going off made the work at her apartment sound like a lullaby.

Val brought Nora to a stop and waited for Neil to put the saw down and reach for a fresh piece of wood. "Look who I found?"

"Surprise." She waved at him and hoped she didn't have a sappy grin on her face.

The shift in his expression from one of concentration to what she could only describe as delight, made her very happy that her day had not gone as planned. "And a nice surprise at that." He put the wood he'd reached for down on the porch and walked over.

"We're off to a great start." Val grinned widely.

Nora didn't see much. The house still looked like it would be a good fit for a bulldozer.

Chuckling quietly, Neil reached for her hand. "Come on in and we'll show you what we're up to. We've gotten quite a bit done the last few days. For starters, the foundation has been reinforced. The old piers are sturdy but we had a few cracked support beams that were replaced. My job has been subfloors and now the front porch. We don't need anyone falling through boards and breaking another ankle."

Foolishly focused on her hand engulfed in his stronger hand, Nora wasn't all too sure what else he'd told her.

The inside of the old house was literally turned upside down. Wood boards and pieces were scattered all about, electric cords snaked through the rooms, tool boxes and saw tables combined to create a challenging obstacle course. It took a few moments of maneuvering through the front room before she realized the big wall between the living area and kitchen was gone. "Oh my."

"Looks different, doesn't it?" Grinning like a little kid, Neil pointed to a stack of newspapers on the floor beside them. "We found these stuffed inside the walls for insulation."

Her gaze drifted over the piles of papers. "Good thing the house never caught on fire. With all of this in the walls it would have gone up like a match on gasoline."

"You'd be amazed how many old houses have newspapers in the walls." Still holding her hand, he leaned over and lifted one of the pages. "Not sure if this was the year the house was built, or if the homeowners went back and redid the walls to improve the insulation, but all these papers are dated 1905."

"Oh, how fun." She accepted the page he handed her. Nothing of major importance seemed to be on the page, but still, the idea of a hundred year plus history was hard to resist. Even as she put the page down on top of the pile, she knew she was going to look through each and every piece of paper, just in case.

"Yes. Isn't it?" Val looked quite pleased with herself. "The discovery made for interesting film during demolition. I'll be going through them and seeing if we can't film another small clip of interest to the viewers. I'm hoping to find something fun and juicy in there."

Nora bet her friend was indeed hoping for something dripping with interesting gossip.

Valerie slapped her hands together and rubbed vigorously. "I don't know about you guys, but I'm starved. Shall we call lunch?"

Neil nodded and one of the workers yelled out what time they were resuming and everyone was off to the food truck. She didn't know about the walls, floors, and newspapers, but she did know that so far, today was turning out to be a great day.

The last thing Neil expected to see on the porch today was Nora. When he looked up from sawing the replacement boards for the crumbling front porch, he had to blink hard to make sure she was really there.

"Do not tell Frank, but this is the best brisket taco I think I have ever had." Nora wiped at a drop of sauce from the corner of her mouth. "I mean, if I'd known this was the kind of food served on film sets, I might have set my sights on Hollywood instead of nursing school."

Valerie chuckled loudly. "You and a few hundred other waiters in Southern California would have had the same idea."

"I suppose." She took another bite and stuck her tongue out to lick her lips before slowly chewing.

"Wait till you taste the chocolate chip cookies." Valerie shoved a wrapped cookie across the resin picnic table.

"Now these are to die for."

"I'm partial to the pecan shortbread cookie," Neil said. This truck the production company provided was a far cry from the construction site trucks he was used to.

"I think I'll have another." Nora set her hands flat on the table to push to her feet. "Or maybe I'll take another look at that menu."

"I think I'll join you." Neil stood and walked the twenty feet to where the truck was parked to the side of several tables set out for the crew to eat at. Unlike normal lunchtime trucks, this one was parked all day and Molly the truck owner kept it running non stop from late morning till shooting shut down, whatever time that might be. The line was several people deep. If this truck were in a big city, the lines would be never ending.

"What can I get you folks?" Molly was a petite thing, who despite working in a very hot confined area, without help, smiled brightly.

After perusing the menu while waiting, Nora stepped forward. "The fried mac and cheese is seriously tempting, but I can't resist trying the Philly cheesesteak."

"A girl after my own heart. With or without peppers?"

"With please." Nora turned to re-examine the handwritten chalkboard menu. "When you say fresh lemonade, do you mean—"

"Squeeze it right here in the truck." Now the woman was truly beaming.

Nora's smile broadened to match the cook's. "I'll take a lemonade too please."

"Make that two, and I'll have the fried mac and cheese." Neil had come to like a lot of things about Nora in the last weeks but that extra twinkle in her eyes when something caught her fancy or interest was probably the most enjoyable after her smile. "If you like, we could share?"

A smile pulled at her cheeks before she bit it back and shrugged, her eyes still sparkling. "Maybe a taste would be nice."

Settling in at the table again, Neil stabbed at the food

with his fork and dangled it in front of Nora. "First bite."

Those eyes sparkled again and she gladly consumed the morsel and then, eyes closing, moaned. "Oh, better than the state fair. I wonder if Molly would like to move into town when this is over."

"I don't know that the café needs the competition."

Nora waved him off. "There are plenty of folks who could use a fast lunch on the go and wouldn't put even a dent in the café's business. Look how fast the town and outskirts are growing. It's like every city person east of Ft Worth has decided they want a simpler life."

"Maybe." He stabbed another piece for her and by the time the team all began clearing their plates and meandering back to the house, he'd had as much cheesesteak as she'd had mac and cheese.

"I guess I'll have to save the cookie sampling till later." Nora eased out of the bench. "Do you think it would be okay if I stuck around and watched for a bit?"

"More than okay." Neil had no idea how anyone else felt about outsiders on the set and he didn't care. "Especially now that we have the foundation and subfloors reinforced. No risk of falling through again."

"Oh," Val stood with her empty plate in hand, "it was never that bad if you were careful."

"I'll still be careful. I've creamed my ankle once stepping off the Farraday back porch, I'd rather not go down that path again." Halfway up the porch, Nora came to a stop and pointed to the living room ceiling. "Uh, is that leg a new design feature?"

Neil shuffled around her and spotted the booted denim leg that came through the plastered ceiling. "Who the…? Hey, what's going on here?"

"Oh, this old town is the gift that keeps giving. Don't anyone move!" Val spun around on her heel and ran down the steps shouting loudly, "Ted, get in here now. I don't want to miss a second of this. I want it all on film!"

"Nice of you to come back to work." Owen's muffled voice came through the ceiling.

Staring up, Neil hesitated, waiting to see if Owen pulled

his leg up and out on his own or if he needed help. When there was no effort at movement, Neil flipped around and hurried toward the ladder under the attic access, He could hear Val and the cameraman gleefully recording the event and something about having to get Owen to do it again for the camera.

"It's not that hard to fix holes in the ceiling, is it?" Val's voice followed him up the steps, Nora only a few steps behind him. He couldn't figure what the heck happened. Falling through the ceiling was a rookie mistake and Owen might not be a part of the hands on crew under normal circumstances, but he was not a rookie.

"Took y'all long enough to finish lunch," Owen spouted through a fake smile. "I don't dare move."

Balancing on the floor beams, Neil turned to Nora. "Careful. We don't need anyone else falling through the ceiling."

She nodded and slowed her steps. Behind her, another cameraman appeared with Valerie on his heels. "I want it all on film."

So far the cameras hadn't been a real issue for him. He and his brothers had just been going about their jobs and paid no never mind to the cameras, but right about now he wasn't overjoyed to have them filming. Neil carefully walked over to his brother. "What were you doing all the way back here?"

"Checking out why the far bedroom is sagging. Spotted that." Owen slung a thumb over his shoulder. "Pulling it out of the way, I lost my balance and thankfully only one foot went down, but I could use some leverage."

"You got it." Neil stretched out his arm, and hanging on to a support post with the other arm, he helped Owen pull out of the hole.

Val's gleeful words of delight over the incident echoed in the cavernous space. Owen stood on the nearest beam and brushed at his leg.

"You okay? Do we need to make a quick trip to see Brooks?"

"No." Owen shook his head. "Just a few pins and

needles. Y'all took your sweet time at lunch."

"Sorry." Neil glanced across the space. "This attic was empty when we came up here. How did we miss that?"

Owen shrugged. "We were more concerned with the support beams. It's dark in the far corners. I could use a stronger flashlight, but I think that lone trunk is all that's left up here. Doesn't look like there's anything else in that corner but some better lighting will help determine if that trunk is the only souvenir."

"Trunk?" Nora's voice carried with a hint of excitement. "I'm coming through."

"Please be careful," Owen and Neil echoed.

"This isn't the first or last Texas attic I've had to do a balance act across."

"I'll have the crew bring some lights up." Valerie spun about again, and hurried across the beams like sure footed feline, calling downstairs to the first cameraman. "Ted, don't stop filming. I want all of this."

Some of the attic had decking near the opening, but this far back there were only beams. From what Neil could see, the trunk was balanced perfectly across two of them.

"Ooh. This old thing has to have been here forever." Nora gently brushed at the inches of dust, then glancing around spotted a loose board nearby and sliding it over, sank to her knees on it.

"Careful," Neil repeated. He did not want her falling.

"I just want a quick look." Her eyes danced with delight at the recent discovery. "I hope it's not locked."

Both Neil and Owen stood over her shoulder. The second cameraman remained to one side. One lonesome trunk. Neil couldn't help but wonder why would whoever had lived here leave this one lonesome trunk behind?

CHAPTER TWELVE

Squeezing the latch, Nora heard a click and popped it open lifting the lid on the newly found treasure. "Oh, wow. It's full to the brim."

"It's pretty dark up here." Neil held his cell phone flashlight over the newly found trunk. "What is it?"

Nora reverently pulled out the first item. Neatly folded, she lifted the corners. "This is in pristine shape."

"Ooh." As quickly as Valerie had rushed out of the attic in search of her crew, she was already back and at Nora's side. "This is an amazing find. We're going to have to film a segment on this somewhere besides a dusty dark attic."

"What about the Mercantile?" the cameraman suggested. "Never hurts to bring in previous work."

"Excellent idea!" Valerie rubbed her hands together and turned to the trunk. "Shall we carry it down?"

Nora looked to Neil. "It is rather dirty up here."

"Agreed, but juggling this thing while walking the balance beam is not the best idea. Give me a few minutes to drop some plywood and we'll bring it down."

Everyone nodded and Valerie led the way out of the attic while Neil and the guys brought up a few sheets of wood to lay temporary decking. They'd carried the old trunk more easily across the attic and were halfway down the steps when a chorus of "Yoo hoo" carried softly from the front of the house.

"Are we throwing a party?" Owen lowered his voice for only his brother to hear.

Neil cocked his head to one side. "Starting to look like it."

Neither of the brothers looked terribly thrilled to have

more people invading their construction site, but Nora didn't care, she was giddy with delight, ready to explore this new find.

In the living room, Sissy stood hands on her hips at her sister's side. "Thought we'd save you a trip into the store with those newspapers you've collected and while we're here check out if Molly's food truck is as good as word around town says it is."

"It is." Nora nodded. "Seriously delicious."

"What's that?" Pointing at the trunk, Sister's eyes rounded wide to match her figure.

"We found it in the attic." Owen gestured with his chin toward the front door. "Let's get this out of here so y'all can scavenge and the rest of us can get back to work."

"Right. Back of my truck?" Neil asked.

Owen nodded and everyone scurried after the two brothers like they were about to toss money from the back of the pickup.

"It's all yours." Owen brushed his hands and turned away. "I have a ceiling to fix."

"And I have a porch to finish." Neil slowed at Nora's side. "Up for dinner tonight?"

Nora nodded.

"Good. Don't leave without letting me know."

"I won't." Her heart was doing a little jig. This pretend thing was feeling a little too real and a lot nice.

Done tinkering with the video camera now pointed at the trunk, the cameraman looked up. "Ready when you are."

"This is so exciting," Sister squealed. "A time capsule and being on television, what more could a girl ask for? But shouldn't one of the good looking guys be here?"

Val glanced at Nora and sighed. "She's right. We really should have at least one of the cousins out here. This is how we're going to play it. You two ladies are going to pretend the cousins have pulled up to the Mercantile with this new discovery. Nora, since you're dating one of the cousins, it brings a more personal element. Everyone loves a hint of romance. I still want you nearby. Of course, everyone will have to sign waivers, but that's for later. For now, no one touch anything until I come back with a cousin."

All heads nodded and Valerie hurried up the porch steps two at a time, stopping first at Neil who nodded, then called into the house. She quickly returned while two good-looking Farradays shared a few words. Wondering what was taking so long, Nora almost cracked up laughing when she realized the two brothers were doing Rock Paper Scissors, probably to see who would be taken away from work and dragged into a walk through history. The new question as Neil trotted down the steps was whether he won or lost.

Gingerly popping the lid open once more, Nora gently fingered the old quilt. "I'm not sure I've ever seen a truly handsewn quilt before. The stitching on this is amazingly tight. Like a sewing machine."

At first, Neil stood quietly to one side. When Valerie cleared her throat, loudly, he stretched out his arms for Nora to hand off the old quilt. "This house is certainly full of surprises," he muttered for the benefit of the camera.

Sissy took a long minute to gently examine the blanket. "Quilting was not only a common pastime back in the day, it was a way of life. Recycling old clothes and keeping warm at night."

"Oh my." Sister leaned forward. "Look at those napkins. They're hand embroidered."

Sissy reached for one. "My mother used to have table linens that belonged to her grandmother, but through the generations of family dinners, stains, and washings, they practically disintegrated. These are like new." She added the napkins and tablecloth to the pile in Neil's arms.

"Do you think this is a wedding dress?" Nora held up a dainty floor length pale blue dress. Simple in cut and design, she was pretty sure the lace, like everything else so far, was hand done.

"If it is," Sissy studied the dress, "that would make it pre Queen Victoria."

"That's right." Sister nodded. "White didn't become popular till after the royal wedding."

"Whoever it belonged to, I wonder if they ever got to

use any of this?"

"Odds are if it's all still here and so nice and neat," Sissy fingered the side of the trunk, "I'm going to guess probably not."

That thought made Nora sad. For someone to have filled a chest with hopes for their future and not only didn't get to use it, but to have those dreams relegated to a deep corner of a forgotten attic. "Do you think there's any way to find out who owned this house?"

Outside of camera view and probably any microphones, Valerie shrugged. "Except for the Parlor House, I don't believe any of the area properties have descendants with claims."

"That would be a shame." Nora really wished somewhere there could be a happy ending for the owner of this old trunk. Then again, even in today's modern world of convenience and communication, no one was guaranteed a happy ever after.

As much as Neil had grumbled about this entire ghost town television project, and about having to step in for Morgan in the day to day work, today was one more reason why he was really, really glad to be involved. Having Nora show up unexpectedly had been a bright spot in a hot Texas morning. Watching her face light up with delight at each delicate item she extricated from the ancient trunk had been the highlight of his day. And the best part of it all was that the day wasn't over.

At the end of the workday, he'd hurried home, taken a record fast shower, and was counting the minutes until he pulled up at Nora's. He had no idea how much longer she was willing to keep up the pretense of dating, but until then he was trying his best to simply enjoy her company. He couldn't remember the last time he enjoyed just hanging out with a member of the opposite sex without any, er, benefits. Simply having her in the same room made the room a nice place to be. And wasn't he sounding ridiculously poetic. Anyone would say he was a love sick teen. He really needed to get a grip. It was only dinner.

Taking an extra minute to check out the surroundings, Neil pulled into a parking space in front of Nora's building. The town seemed so peaceful. He loved this time of the evening. No longer day, not quite night, life slowing down, and now, dinner with Nora.

He slammed his door shut and made it halfway to her door when it flew open and Nora stepped out. "Heard you pull up. I think your truck needs a new muffler."

"It needs a new lot of things." He chuckled. One of these days he'd get around to picking out something new, but for now, his old truck worked just fine.

"Café or pub?" She slid into the front seat and he closed the door behind her.

"Frank's special for tonight is his meatloaf and I have it on good authority that Jamie made corned beef and cabbage tonight. Which strikes your fancy?"

"Not fair," she grinned, "both are delicious and you know it."

He smiled and cocked his head. "They are, but the decision is yours."

"I'm a sucker for Jamie's corned beef. Besides," she nibbled softly on the corner of her mouth, "I wouldn't mind running into Emily again."

"I wouldn't mind running into her again myself."

"Oh." The look on her face told him very quickly she'd misunderstood his intent.

"Don't mind her being around when I show off my best girl."

Nora laughed. "I swear, you could charm the rattles off a snake. Thank you."

"I'm going to take that as a compliment."

"Please do."

The moment they crossed the threshold of the pub, the hostess hurried over to them. "Take any seat you want. We're a little short staffed tonight. I keep telling Jamie if he's going to make his corned beef he needs to bring in extra help even if this is only Thursday night."

"It does seem to be a brisk business, doesn't it?" Nora glanced around.

He wondered if she was looking for the corner table too. Unfortunately, someone had beat them to the somewhat private spot. "How about over there?"

Following the direction of his finger, Nora nodded and they crossed to the two-top table against the far wall. Usually if Jamie had live entertainment, it was on Friday or Saturday when the crowds were larger and stayed longer, but tonight looked like it was going to be an exception. Setting up on stage, a young girl pulled out her guitar and adjusted the microphone. Within a few minutes, the dull roar of chatter in the place had softened to listen to the young girl.

"She's really good." Neil hadn't expected such a powerful voice from such a petite thing, and her repertoire of classic tunes made popular by seventies pop stars like James Taylor and Cat Stevens was equally surprising.

"That's Nicole Brady. She's been singing at church parties since she was no taller than her guitar. I didn't realize she'd graduated to performing outside of church."

"She's good enough to be performing anywhere she wants." He couldn't help but tap his fingers to the beat. Before the girl was done with her set, Neil and Nora and half the audience were singing along.

"Don't turn around, but look who just walked in." The satisfied smile on Nora's face told him all he needed to know about who had come through the front door.

Sure enough, Emily stopped at the table with the average looking guy Neil had learned was Emily's husband. Nothing extraordinary about him, other than his banking career. Apparently Emily lauded her name and her jewelry around town like a queen reigning over her subjects.

"I see you're both still together."

Something about the way Emily sneered the words made Neil want to say something, anything, to put the woman in her place. Instead he took advantage of the slow swaying tune and grabbed Nora's hand. "If you'll excuse us, this is a favorite song and we were just about to dance."

"Oh, of course." Emily stepped back, her expression startled. Probably that anyone would walk away from the queen while she was holding court.

On the floor, he twirled Nora into his arms and held her just a little closer than he might have under normal circumstances. "Is this okay? Am I holding you too tight?"

"Perfectly okay," was all she said.

At first, he could feel the eyes boring into his back, but with every beat of the song he lost track of all things around him and simply swayed to the rhythms only they could make. The song came to an end, another began, and they remained in place, slowly moving to the soft soulful tune. One hand on the small of her back, the other hand holding hers close to his shoulder, they effortlessly glided around the floor as if they'd been dancing together all their lives. Nicole announced she was taking a short break and Neil didn't want to leave the floor, didn't want to stop, and most importantly, didn't want to let go of this woman who fit so perfectly in the fold of his arms. There was no doubt in his mind, continuing this little charade was like playing with fire in a haystack.

"I guess we should go sit down now?" Nora had taken a half step back and stared up into his eyes.

"Probably." His gaze shifted to the other side of the room where he noticed Emily seated with her husband, the woman's eyes set clearly on him and Nora. The canned music began playing overhead. A popular tune he recognized but couldn't put his finger on. A song perfect for one more dance. Without asking, he pulled her in against him again and began once again moving around the small space.

The dance floor had grown more crowded as another song came on. He spotted Emily out of the corner of his eye dragging her husband out to join the other dancers. When Emily finally won the battle and planted herself and her other half only inches away from Neil and Nora, his left hand released its hold on her hand and gently caressed the line of her jaw. "Let's give Emily something to really talk about."

He waited a beat and when Nora gave a half bob of her head, he let his lips come down to meet hers. More than a peck, and probably more than he should have dared, but he couldn't stop himself, and yet, he had no choice. Grudgingly pulling back, he took hold of her hand again and resumed dancing around the floor. Who was he really fooling? Emily Taub or himself?

CHAPTER THIRTEEN

Not for the first time today, Nora's mind wandered off to last night's toe tingling kiss. A stack of folders were all filed while she mentally revisited dancing in Neil's arms. Not till she'd cleared her desk did she realize that half the folders had not been updated and were not ready for filing. Reliving how perfectly she seemed to fit against him, she absently gave Neil Farraday an appointment at noon next Thursday instead of correctly attributing the appointment in the calendar to Mrs. Thompson. Now when she was supposed to be concentrating on the task at hand, she was lost in wanting to skip girls' night at the B&B and go dancing again with Neil, and if she were lucky enough, get another sizzling goodnight kiss.

"You seem a bit distracted." One of the lab techs stopped at her desk. "I hope it's nothing serious."

Nora shook her head. "Just one of those days. Can't seem to concentrate."

"You probably need more sleep. I've started taking melatonin gummies. I think they're helping me sleep more soundly."

"You think?"

The tech shrugged and smiled. "Jury is still out."

"Got it." Nora smiled back at her. "But I sleep just fine, thanks." At least she had up until last night. She'd tossed and turned and her mind had played games of forget me nots and spin the bottle as if she were still a hormonal teen who could easily crush on her good looking classmates.

"Does the doc have any more appointments this afternoon?"

"Nope." Nora glanced up at the clock. Thirty minutes till quitting time. She was looking forward to hanging out with her friends. Friday nights with the girls was always a guaranteed fun night. Maybe that would help her stop thinking about Neil. The man had a way of slipping into her thoughts and dreams and staying there.

"I think it's safe to close up early." Brooks tapped his ring on the edge of the doorway. "If anyone walks in, I can handle it."

That idea sounded wonderful. She wasn't doing a very good job with her work anyhow. If she wasted too much more time she might have to re-file the entire office once she stopped woolgathering over Neil. "I think that's a great idea. Thanks."

Opening her bottom desk drawer, she pulled out her purse and pushed to her feet.

"See you at church Sunday."

She nodded, waved, and hurried out the door. With her extra time she could stop at the market and pick up some snack food. She came across what looked like an easy recipe for a crab dip. Hopefully if she could keep her mind on task, she wouldn't burn the darn thing.

One crab dip and fresh change of clothes later and she was ready for a night of old movies and good friends. She briefly considered walking to the B&B, but decided as pleasant a night as it was at the moment, a few hours from now might not be the same.

Judging from the crowd of cars parked up and down the street, the turnout must be good. She grabbed the dip and bounced up the steps. "Honey, I'm home," she called out teasingly.

"We're in the kitchen," Meg called back.

Her assumptions had been correct. The kitchen was packed.

"Look at this guy." Kate, a vet tech from the clinic and a recent member of the ladies night group, held her phone out for everyone to see. "Not only is he funny looking, but the comment about nothing more beautiful than the female body is kind of creepy."

Meg looked over Kate's shoulder and shuddered. "That's more than creepy."

"Are you still trying to find the perfect match online?" Becky grabbed a bowl of chips from the table. "I have a friend from college who met her husband online. Now she lives on a sheep ranch in Montana."

Kate lifted her gaze from her phone. "Is she happy?"

"Actually," Becky chuckled, "I think so. But there were some doozies before she found him."

"I know." Shannon refilled her drink. "I am so glad I'm not in the dating game anymore. We've got this new young waitress at the diner who is practically addicted to those dating apps. She's always on her phone. Always chatting with strange guys, and the worst part is always sharing it with the rest of us trying to work."

"Don't tell Abbie that." Aunt Eileen stuck her head in the fridge and pulled out a tray of Toni's cake balls. "The last thing she needs is a distracted waitress."

"She already knows. It's weird how twenty year olds are so good at using their phones while juggling real lives." Shannon sighed. "If anything happened to Brad I don't think I could deal with the hassle of the meat market again, whether online or in person. It all feels so exhausting. I just really feel badly for singles who have to find someone nowadays."

"I know what you mean." Grace grabbed a bowl of freshly popped popcorn and shook it with her famous garlic butter and parmesan concoction. "Not everyone can have a dog match them up with a big city escapee."

"Comedian." Meg smacked her sister in law on the bottom. "I'm just glad I found Adam before I even had to think about dating again. Not that before Adam, no matter how I met them, my choice in men was all that great."

And this little conversation cemented Nora's determination to keep her failed online dating attempts from her friends. She was sure they would be gracious and supportive because that's just who they all were, but she was also sure deep down they'd feel sorry for her having to resort to online dating.

"If my dating history teaches us anything it's that there's someone for everyone, it just sometimes might take longer than we like. So," Meg slapped her hands together and brushed them enthusiastically, "it's going to be a great night with friends. We've got so much delicious junk food that we might be able to stay and keep eating till next Friday."

That made Nora and a handful of other ladies laugh. "I hope there isn't too much food. I brought crab dip, but I need to warm it up first."

"Oh my." Grace gawked at the large bowl Nora carried. "I love anything crab."

"Then you're in luck. It turned out pretty darn good, if I do say so myself."

"Did someone say crab?" Becky came in from the other room, an empty glass in hand. "The movie is all prepped, and Aunt Eileen is standing guard over the popcorn. We'd better get started."

Maybe she was being unexpectedly self conscious, but Nora was almost one hundred percent convinced all heads in the room turned to her as soon as she walked into the den.

"It's about time you got here." Allison scooted onto the edge of her seat. "Rumors have been flying all over town and I don't get enough time off to wait and see. Tell us exactly what is going on with you and Neil?"

Wasn't that a loaded question.

"Emily Taub told Polly that you two looked awfully cozy last night at the pub." Allison dropped a kernel of popcorn in her mouth and waited as if Nora were the evening entertainment.

"There's not much to tell."

"That's not what I heard." Becky sunk into a nearby chair. "Might as well spill it because if we don't hear the truth, the rest of the town will make something up."

"I'm not kidding. We've been out together a few times. He's nice."

"Nice?" Meg chuckled. "Is that really all you can say?"

"He's very nice?" she tried again.

"Just remember," Aunt Eileen smiled, "when a Farraday falls, he falls hard."

"I don't think you have to worry about that." Nora did her best to flash a casual smile. There was no way she could tell everyone in the room this whole spending time together was nothing more than a silly idea to make her look good in front of people like Emily Taub and save herself a little embarrassment. She knew he was expecting her to step back after putting on a show for a little while, but she wasn't in any hurry. Spending time one on one with Neil was far from a hardship. And she sure as heck wouldn't mind some more of those toe tingling kisses. Whenever she was with him, he made her feel special. Whether it was walking through town, climbing in an attic, or dancing after dinner. Maybe he made her feel special because he was special.

"Earth to Nora." Meg waved her hand in front of Nora. "I recognize that look. Used to see it in the mirror every morning. You've been bitten by the Farraday love bug."

Ready to speak up and insist Meg was wrong, Nora snapped her mouth shut when Toni spun around in her seat and waved an arm at Nora. "What did the dogs say?"

"The dogs?" Shannon asked. "You're kidding?"

"No." Toni shook her head adamantly. "I'm dead serious. Those dogs haven't been wrong yet."

Meg bobbed her head and waved a pointed finger at Toni. "I agree. Has anyone seen those dogs hanging around Nora or Neil?"

A deep frown formed between Aunt Eileen's brows, and Nora knew that the Farraday matriarch was considering the possibility of a Farraday match without the canine approval. Aunt Eileen believed in the matchmaking powers of the dogs as much as Meg, Toni, and half the town. Maybe more.

"Dog or no dog," Allison waved a finger at Nora, "every single woman in town is green with envy."

Wasn't that a laugh worthy comment. She was just as jealous of herself as everyone else. Every day she had to remind herself none of this was real, except last night on the dance floor, whatever charade they were playing felt very real. So real, that at this very minute, like it or not, she was the one falling hard for a Farraday.

"I'm in Tuckers Bluff," Neil's brother Ryan snapped his fingers at Neil. "But where are you?"

"What?" Neil knew he'd been zoning out all through dinner, but that was no reason for his brother to be singling him out now.

"You may have been sitting in the dining room, but your mind was most definitely somewhere else. I know you're not a chatty Kathy, but still, you were awfully quiet. Especially after Owen brought up the trunk."

"Actually," Neil chuckled and took a short swallow of his beer, "I found Owen falling through the ceiling much more entertaining."

Morgan didn't try to hide his laughter. "I'd have paid good money to have been there to see that." He dropped one hand behind his calf to massage his injured leg. "It's not like him to make a stupid mistake like that. Any idea if something is eating at him too?"

"Too?"

"Well, it's not like you to be quiet and tonight if you uttered an entire sentence it was a lot. I can't make up my mind which one of you is more out of sorts."

"No big deal with me. I've got a lot on my mind. It's not fun designing and rehabbing a house by committee."

"Committee?"

"You know. The town council, the developers, the production company and let's not forget the sisters. Those two have plenty of ideas."

"I bet they do, but it's no worse than having a wife and husband on two opposite sides of the drawing board and an interfering relative or two on top of that." Morgan continued rubbing his leg and glanced over the porch railing to the dark night ahead. "At least you're not falling through ceilings. He could have broken his neck."

Neil nodded, delighted to have the heat on someone else. He did not want to spend the rest of the evening discussing his unusual relationship with Nora. One that he wanted to shift from fake to real and didn't have a clue how to go about it. For now, picking on his knucklehead ceiling crashing brother was a great alternative. "Owen does seem to be a bit distracted."

"He claims he lost his balance tugging on the trunk, but he's not usually that uncoordinated." Morgan continued rubbing his leg and staring into the distance. "I suppose I should be thankful Pax and Ryan aren't acting weird too."

Gray came meandering up the path and onto the porch, nuzzled up against Morgan for a quick ear scratch then went and laid at Neil's feet. "You create a lot of commotion for a cattle dog."

"You don't believe those rumors, do you?" Morgan stopped rubbing his leg and leaned back in the rocker. "He's just a smart dog."

As if displeased by the comment, Gray huffed and shook his head to one side before resting his head on the deck again and staring Morgan down.

"Don't look at me that way." Morgan frowned. "I said you were smart."

The dog huffed again with what could have passed for a groan if he'd been human.

"I don't think you're going to win this argument."

"Where's his other half?" Morgan looked up and down the porch and over the railing.

"I think she went with Aunt Eileen to girls night."

"Really? Since when does Aunt Eileen take the dogs with her?"

"Since the women have been a bit spooked by DJ's updates on how they're not catching what is clearly a serial rapist."

"It's not like Aunt Eileen hangs out at bars looking to hook up."

"And neither do any of the other ladies we know from town, but the idea of something so ugly so close to home has everyone a little on edge. So she takes a dog with her wherever she goes lately and neither of these two seem to complain."

"They are good dogs. Dad would love a pair like this."

"And Mom would have a cow if he tried to bring them into the house." Neil leaned over to scratch at the dog's ears. "Have you ever thought about what brought Mom and Dad together?"

"I don't know. What brings any two people together?"

"Don't get me wrong, Mom's a great woman and we all love her, but she's really different from Aunt Eileen and Aunt Anne."

"How so?"

"For one thing," Neil ticked off a finger, "Mom is more reserved than they are. Everything seems to be about rules with her, but not so much with our aunts. Then another thing is Uncle Sean and Uncle Brian worked hard to keep the family tied together and I get the feeling Dad would have liked to but Mom not so much. Can you picture Aunt Eileen letting anything come between her family members?"

Morgan shook his head. "Aunt Anne is a bit of a protective tigress herself."

"And Brian and Sean are only cousins, not brothers, and yet all their kids behave like siblings."

"I know." Morgan returned his gaze to the land beyond the barns. "Should I be worried about you and Owen? I don't want to see anything break us all up."

Neil shook his head. "I promise you, there is nothing going on in my life that's going to drive a wedge between us. I may pull a few hairs out of my head before we're done with this TV gig," and he might lose more than a few night's sleep thinking about Nora, "but y'all aren't getting rid of me that easily."

A slow easy grin took over Morgan's face. "Ya think this whole TV thing is getting to Owen too?"

Hefting one shoulder in a lazy shrug, Neil shook his head. "You mean besides the tight budget we saddled him with? Don't know, but I'm sure if there's something important, he would come tell us."

"Hm," Morgan huffed. "We'll see."

Now Morgan had him wondering about Owen. So distracted by his own life and challenges, Neil hadn't paid much attention to whether any of his brothers were acting out of character. And while his gut instinct was to insist everyone was fine, right now he wasn't all that confident in instincts he'd trusted for years. "Maybe we should ask Pax."

"I already did. He doesn't know anything."

Neil nodded. While Ryan and Quinn were Irish twins born eleven months apart, Paxton and Owen were identical twins. If something were seriously wrong with Owen, even if no one else knew anything, Pax would know if something was up with his twin.

"Hey, you two anti-socials," Finn teased. "Dad's breaking out the cards. Up for a little Texas Hold 'em?"

Morgan nodded. "Good idea. I'm getting tired of thinking."

"You and me both." Neil pushed to his feet. He doubted even a friendly card game with his family would be enough to keep Nora off his mind, but it was certainly worth a try. All he had to decide tonight was whether or not he would call Nora and invite her to dinner tomorrow night, or bide his time till Sunday dinner.

CHAPTER FOURTEEN

It had taken everything in Nora Sunday morning after church to turn down the polite invitation to dinner at the Farradays. Aside from how much she enjoyed time at the ranch, she enjoyed time with Neil more than she should. All night Friday she'd tossed and turned and then spent the better part of Saturday debating what to do about Neil. By Sunday morning she hadn't reached a single bloody conclusion and opted to skip the family dinner.

It was no surprise that she hadn't heard from anyone on Monday and now that Brooks' weekly house call day had rolled around, Nora had to decide if heading out to the construction site was a good or bad idea.

Sitting alone in the office could lead to two things. Either catching up on all the paperwork that had piled up during a very distracted week, or more likely, wasting the day remembering all her time spent with Neil and thinking how sweet it would all be if it weren't just for show. She could not remember for the life of her if any man she'd ever known had made her laugh as easily as Neil did, or made her feel as special as a royal princess. And for sure not since her giddy years in high school did a guy take up all her spare brain cells. No. She pushed to her feet. Her paperwork would not be caught up today. She was heading out to the homestead. Maybe she'd round someone up from Friday night to join her. Half the girls' night crowd had been excited at the prospect of trying out the food truck, surely she could find one to tag along so she wouldn't look too much like a lovesick puppy chasing after Neil.

Lovesick. The word stuck in her mind, repeating itself like a never-ending mantra. Grabbing her handbag, she shook her head and decided she was thinking too much and too hard. Pushing all thoughts aside and listening only to her growling stomach, she was on a mission.

The doors secured, keys in hand, she'd made it down the front steps when she almost bumped into Polly rushing in the direction of her salon. "I'm so sorry. I wasn't looking where I was going."

"No problem. Totally my fault. I was in a hurry to get lunch."

"We're splurging for Frank's meatball parmesan heroes, and if I don't get these back while they're still warm, I'll never hear the end of it." Polly held up both arms holding brown paper sacs and continued up the block walking backwards. "By the way, congrats on you and Neil."

"Thanks. You go. Enjoy." Now that so many people believed they were an item, it was probably time to do her part and become an item-no-more. Or maybe it would be okay to stretch this out just a little longer. Determination to head out to the homestead faded as she considered the looming deadline and Frank's famed meatball parmesan sandwiches. How obvious would it be to Neil that she was wanting to see him? After all, how stupid would she look going all the way to the truck for lunch? Or maybe he'd think she was out there to play her part. And there she was over thinking again.

A silver mid-sized SUV pulled up to the curb and rolling down the glass, Kelly leaned over and called through the window. "I was just coming to see what you're doing for lunch. Adam gave me the afternoon off and I've been hankering for the food truck lunches you raved about."

"Funny you should say that. I've been daydreaming about the food truck menu all morning." And a few other things she wasn't going to mention.

"Great. Climb in and we'll head out."

"Deal." Nora eagerly climbed into the car. She was ready for a change of pace and more importantly, a redirection of her thoughts. Buckled in, she settled in for the not too long drive to the homestead construction site. "I'm really glad you thought to stop by and include me."

"I'm glad you're free. Whenever Ian is out of town on an assignment things always feel a little empty, so the company is very much appreciated."

"Is he going to be gone long?"

Kelly shook her head. "Nah, ever since we got married, he's rarely gone more than a few days at a time. I'm expecting him back tonight."

The conversation continued shifting from how much fun Kelly and Ian were having fixing up the old Stemmons' place they'd bought last year, to how the town was growing so much that Adam was seriously looking for a partner to ease the load, to how the whole darn town from corner to corner were practically on the edge of their seats speculating on Nora and Neil's relationship. By the time they pulled into the makeshift parking lot on the outskirts of the property, they laughed themselves silly over some of the family's romantic escapades.

Nora stepped out of the car and slammed the door shut, facing Kelly. "I can still see Jamison diving over the table chasing Gray."

"The whole town remembers that one." Kelly closed her door and fell in step with Nora. "But nothing beats Chase going all *Pretty Woman* on Grace. I still can't get over his flying her all the way to New Orleans for dinner."

"That really did sound awfully romantic."

"Way more so than getting bailed out of jail." Kelly chuckled loudly.

Nora laughed along with her. It had been a crazy end to Finn and Joanna's wedding with Kelly getting arrested.

"Oh my." Kelly stood in front of the truck side menu. "There are way more options than I expected."

"I know. All the more reason why I wanted to come back and try something else on the menu." Nora perused a handwritten chalkboard, happy to beat the crew to an early lunch.

"Glad to see you back." Molly smiled at Nora. "Always appreciate it when customers bring friends."

Even though the lunch rush had not started, Nora could tell from how little beads of sweat were pooling at Molly's temple that she'd been working hard in the hot truck prepping for the inevitable line of workers that would be queuing up any minute. "Your food speaks for itself."

"Thank you." Wiping the sweat with her elbow, Molly turned to deal with something behind her and when she swirled back around she straightened and hid a grimace.

"Long day already?" Nora asked.

The smiling woman shook her head. "Haven't been sleeping well. Probably twisted something in my sleep." Her hand moved from her middle back to her neck. "Might be time for a new pillow too."

"Have you tried the memory foam ones?" Kelly had shifted her attention from the menu to the brief conversation. "At first I thought it was horribly uncomfortable but I haven't had a stiff neck in ages."

"Thanks. I'll have to look into picking one up."

"You're staying at the Parlor B&B with the Sisters, right?"

Molly nodded.

"Just let them know. They'll be able to fix you up."

"Thanks. I'll do that."

Instead of trying something new, Nora settled on the mouthwatering brisket tacos again and sweet potato tots, Kelly ordered the fried mac and cheese that had gotten rave reviews from anyone who had tried it. Waiting, Nora glanced at her watch then across the lot to the homestead. There seemed to be minimal activity outside, so she assumed everybody was working inside. She also hoped they'd be taking a break for lunch soon.

No sooner had she wished the production team to break for lunch then the parade of Farraday brothers and scattered crewmen appeared on the front porch making their way toward her. Only one Farraday caught her eye, and interest. The moment Neil's eyes locked with hers a broad smile crept across his face. The twinkle in those baby blues made her grin back at him. Everything about him made her want to grin.

As he walked up to her, he slowed his steps and when he was directly in front of her, leaned forward and shared a chaste peck on the lips. "Hi."

So surprised by the greeting, she'd almost lost her ability to think. "Hi."

"This is a nice surprise."

"I had a hankering for Molly's cooking."

"Can't blame you. She's great."

"Really." Nora turned to face Molly in time to see her popping a few antacids. If she had already tasted what good cook Molly was, Nora would jump to the conclusion that any chef who needed antacids from their own cooking couldn't be very good.

Momentarily swaying in place, Molly paused from working over the hot grill to rub the side of her neck and run her fingers up her jaw to her temple.

Neil stepped up to the truck side window. He seemed to study Molly a long minute before placing his order. When she confirmed his order would be ready in five minutes, Neil stepped aside and huddled close to Nora. "She doesn't look so good. I think the Texas heat and the confined kitchen heat might be more than she bargained for. Before we go home tonight I'll grab Ryan and see if we can't do something to improve the ventilation in there for her."

"That will be nice, but those antacids she's popping aren't because of the heat. Not in the truck anyway."

"This is Texas, she's probably overdoing the spices."

"Hmm."

"Nora. Order up." Molly flashed a weak smile. "Here you go."

"Thanks." For a short minute, Nora wondered if her traditional cooking skills would be of any value if she were to offer to skip lunch and help Molly out in the kitchen on wheels. Though all she'd be doing is adding one more source of body heat to the already confined kitchen space. Another second later and the pinched look on Molly's face told Nora everything she didn't want to know. "Crap."

Neil had no idea what the heck had just happened. Nora spun away from the window, shoved her dish of food in his hands and sputtering words that would have gotten his mouth washed out with soap as a kid, took off running down the side of the restaurant on wheels.

Worried she might have gotten food poisoning or the flu or who knew what malady that would have her rushing away from people to throw up, he shoved the same plate at his brother and tore off after her. Not wanting to draw attention to her, he hurried after Nora in silence.

When Nora reached the opposite side of the truck, she bolted up the steps and inside. "Molly, I need to take your pulse."

"My what?" The woman cast a fast glance over her shoulder before wiping more sweat away with her sleeve and resuming flipping a couple of burgers the crew had ordered. Neil was no doctor but he understood where Nora's concerns were coming from.

"Pulse," she repeated. "I don't think it's the heat that's getting to you. Are you under a lot of stress?"

"Isn't everyone?" Molly leaned into the window. "Kelly, order up." No sooner had she called out the order and rung the little bell she had nearby, than Molly did a near perfect pirouette before spiraling to the ground.

"Oh, hell." Neil had reached the doorway in time to see Molly's pained expression moments before taking a dive. He watched in total horror and complete awe as Nora placed two fingers on Molly's neck, shook her head. "No pulse." On all fours, she leaned toward the woman.

Immediately, her hands moving at high speed, Nora rolled Molly onto her back and began chest compressions. "Call the hospital. See if we can get an airlift. I think she's having a heart attack."

"Heart attack." It wasn't a question. Neil's mind kicked into high gear. "Do you need a defibrillator?"

"You have one?" Arms board stiff, Nora pressed with the precision measures of a metronome.

He nodded. "We bought an AED not long ago for just this reason."

"Get it. Fast." She paused to lean in again and once more returned to the stiff presses on the petite woman's chest.

Tearing across the parking lot, Neil barked at his brother. "Call Ethan and Brooks. We need transportation for Molly. Nora says she's having a heart attack."

His brother didn't say a word, he merely sprang up from his seat at the nearby picnic table and pulled out his cell.

Neil sprinted up to the construction trailer, threw the door open and taking two steps at a time, quickly opened the cabinet with the first aid emblem on the door. It only took a second to recognize the bright red AED bag.

Murmurs from the crowd that had gathered by the truck, fueled his already hurried pace back to Nora and Molly.

"Here you go." He set the bag down beside her.

"Take over for me."

She didn't even ask if he knew how, and thank heaven he did. Sliding into her space, on his knees, he continued the steady paced compressions as Nora opened the bag.

With practiced efficiency, she removed the clear plastic cover and pressed the sticky side of the pads against Molly's chest. She waited for the machine to analyze her heart rhythm. As they'd expected, the machine advised shocking the heart into normal rhythm.

"Stand back. All clear," Nora ordered, waiting until he moved back before pushing the button to send a much needed shock into her heart. For a moment Nora's eyes moved from Molly to the monitor and back again.

Still no response. "Again, all clear."

His heart lodged in his throat as she pushed the button to shock Molly again. The seconds dragged by with excruciating slowness. Once more she repeated the steps, this time the machine showing a steady rhythm, only Nora didn't look any happier as she muttered through clenched teeth, "Damn it."

If he was reading the machine correctly, Molly's heart was beating. "What's wrong?"

"She's still not breathing." Leaning over the deadly still body, Nora began puffing breaths into the woman's lungs.

The air in the room grew thick and heavy and those four words from Nora's lips had Neil's own heart aching for the woman lying helpless on the floor. He barely knew Molly, but she was always smiling and joking with the crew. Everyone really liked her. The idea of a heart simply stopping in someone so young left him numb.

Footsteps landed loud and hard up to the too tiny space. Owen popped his head inside. "Ryan says Ethan will be here in ten. Brooks suggested you might need this." His brother held out the portable oxygen equipment, including a face mask and tubing connected to a green cylinder.

Not too many years ago one of their crew had suffered a massive heart attack on a construction site and the portable external defibrillator and portable oxygen cylinder were the only things that saved the man's life. Ever since, working so often far from big city hospitals, they had made it a point to keep all available emergency first aid equipment, no matter the cost, on every construction site. Never had he been more thankful for the day the brothers had agreed the expense was necessary.

"She's breathing on her own now." Nora heaved a deep sigh and softly murmured, "Thank you, Father."

He couldn't have said it better himself. While he was thankful for the equipment and the oxygen, and for not losing such a sweet young woman, he would add one more thing to the list. Thank heaven for Nora Brown.

CHAPTER FIFTEEN

Saving lives was something one expected to happen, hoped to happen, when a person went into the medical profession. As was losing lives. But when Nora had set off for a luncheon adventure with Kelly, having to save a life had not been on her agenda. Once Ethan arrived with the air flight helicopter team, Nora stepped aside and as soon as the helo lifted off the ground her strength plummeted. Had Neil not been standing next to her, she probably would have just sat right on the dust covered ground.

Arms weak from compressions, she was thankful she'd ridden with Kelly and wouldn't have to drive herself home. A long soak in a hot bathtub had sounded good. The invitation to dinner at the ranch that Aunt Eileen refused to accept a no for had sounded even better. Neil had insisted on driving her to the ranch, and since Ian was coming home tonight Nora didn't feel badly letting Kelly drive home alone. The way Neil had been hovering over her since the incident, anyone would think she'd been the one to have a heart attack.

They'd barely crossed the threshold of the Farraday ranch house when Aunt Eileen came rushing out from the kitchen. "Our hero of the day!"

The woman's hug was so tight and comforting that Nora felt almost instantly rejuvenated. "I wouldn't go that far."

"I would." Neil hung his hat on a nearby hook. "You spotted she was in distress when nobody else did. Then when she collapsed you knew it was a heart attack. I honestly would've thought it was heatstroke or heat exhaustion or any number of other things. I would never have thought that someone as young as her could have a heart attack. Without you there, she would have died."

Having already heard that Molly was expected to recover with no ill affects had been music to Nora's ears. Days like this restored her soul to fight another day. "The truth is stress will kill you at any age. One of the crew was telling me that Molly worked multiple jobs to save for her own truck and now she works seven days a week to keep it profitable."

"Seven?" Aunt Eileen frowned.

Neil nodded. "She goes to Poplar Springs for the farmers market on Saturday and the flea market on Sunday. And she goes to Butler Springs on Friday nights for their Food Trucks Dinner at the Park events."

"Good grief." Sean Farraday came out from his office. "A schedule like that would give anyone a heart attack."

Owen and Ryan came in the door behind them. "Any updates on Molly?"

"So far she's in the cardiac unit, stable, and expected to make a full recovery." Aunt Eileen shook her head. "But Brooks promised to let me know when we can pay her a visit."

The back door slammed shut and pausing to brush his boots and hang his hat, Finn joined them in the living room. "I heard y'all had an exciting day."

"I could do without any more days with that kind of excitement." Neil looked to the back door as it squeaked open again.

This time Connor and Catherine came in followed by Finn's wife Joanna. All the people made Nora want to smile. This was just one of the reasons she loved the Farraday home. As an only child, so many family members in one place, and knowing they all had each other's backs under any circumstance, was something she envied. Being accepted as one of them and having their support and comfort, and friendship, was something she treasured.

"We might as well get comfortable." Aunt Eileen gestured to the sofas. "Dinner's going to be a while."

Nora sat on the corner of the sofa and watched contentedly as all the siblings and cousins and in-laws shifted about grabbing drinks and making themselves comfortable.

Handing her a glass of white wine, Neil took a seat beside her. "I know I'm repeating myself, but you really were amazing today."

"Just doing what I was trained for."

"Doesn't matter. I do every day what I'm trained for, and there's nothing amazing about it."

"That's not true. Taking a dilapidated shack and turning it into a happy home is very much amazing."

The front door swung open and DJ and Becky strolled in. Becky sported her standard bright smile, but DJ carried the weight on his shoulders that showed on his face.

"Do I smell lasagna?" DJ sniffed at the air.

Aunt Eileen stood in the kitchen archway, wiping her hands with a towel. "You do. And it won't be ready for another half hour so help yourself to something to drink."

"You go ahead and sit." Becky kissed her husband on the cheek. "I'll bring you back a beer."

DJ shook his head. "I'll just have a cola."

Casually, Becky squeezed her husband's hand and nodded. "Coming right up."

The family patriarch leaned forward in his seat. "Another victim?"

No one had to ask victim of what or if they'd caught the guy they'd been chasing now for weeks.

DJ nodded. "Butler Springs again."

"Anything new to go on?" his father asked.

"I wish I could say I'm not allowed to share, but truth is no. We keep eliminating suspects and options but don't feel any closer now than we did a week ago."

His father shook his head. "Eliminating possibilities may not feel any closer, but it is. You'll get this guy. I know y'all will."

Nora could see from the look in DJ's eyes that he wasn't ready to agree. The search for this guy was weighing heavily on him and his police force. All crime was repugnant in so many ways, but some like this were downright abhorrent.

"If not for the other cities struck, the common denominator would be the Boot N Scoots. Except for three, most of the victims remembered going to the Boot N Scoots and woke up in a strange motel room, all within walking distance of the dance hall. One motel in particular seems to be this guy's preference."

"Do you have the managers looking out for him?" Connor came in with his wife and dropped on the loveseat.

"Some of these places rent by the hour. Not known for their security vigilance."

"Mm. I see what you mean." Connor sighed.

Joanna pulled up a chair near her husband. "Do you think it's got a connection with some dating apps? You know, like that crime wave a while back getting their victims from ride share apps."

The mere mention of dating apps had Nora almost cringing. Neil either noticed the tension that had suddenly gripped her or was thinking back to how they met. Nonetheless, he'd reached over and easily grabbed hold of her hand and squeezed. When she lifted her gaze from her engulfed hand to his face, deep blue eyes bore down on her. He might as well have wrapped her in a warm blanket. She really was going to miss when this charade was over.

Nora didn't have to say a word. Neil could see the discomfort in her eyes when Joanna sat down next to Finn and brought up the dating apps. With every passing day, and every new thing he learned about Nora Brown, the more he had come to understand that this little arrangement for appearance sake was no longer pretend for him. Now he just had to find the right time and place to convince her to give him a try for real.

"Isn't it possible to do some sort of sting?" Aunt Eileen stood between the two rooms, her gaze shifting from the family conversation to the sauce simmering on the stove.

From the archway that separated the foyer and dining room, with silverware in her hands, Catherine paused from setting the table to join the conversation. "That's what I was wondering. I know this may seem a bit simplistic from a former corporate attorney, but stings not only work with orchestrated tv shows, they bring down bad guys in real life."

DJ nodded. "If we had the manpower to pull off an operation like we might've done back in Dallas or Chicago, but not only do our counties not have huge budgets, you know that we're spread really thin across a lot of territory."

The Farraday siblings, who side-by-side through the years had seen the struggles of DJ's job, understood the truth of his statement and defeatedly nodded their heads.

"All other challenges aside, we simply don't have enough women on the force. Esther in dispatch is the only female in our department and she doesn't fit the victim's profile."

Still standing under the archway, Catherine sighed and shook her head. "I get what you're saying, but you think for all the disadvantages of a small town police force that you have to deal with, the simple fact that these are small towns should be an advantage. Can you imagine what it's like to find a serial rapist in a city like New York or Chicago?"

"Or Dallas." DJ's expression remained stone-faced, and pretty much everyone in the room knew they didn't want to think about some of the atrocities that he'd most likely faced on the big city police force before coming home.

A buzzer sounded in the kitchen and Aunt Eileen spun around. "Dinner's ready. I need a few hands in the kitchen. Everyone else to the table."

Nora stood with the others and turned toward the kitchen and with those crazy eyes on the back of her head, Aunt Eileen called over her shoulder, "Guest of honor doesn't do kitchen duty."

"I'm the guest of honor? And all these years I thought I was just a friend," Nora teased.

Neil leaned into her. "You are to me."

"Anyone ever notice how no matter the situation, eventually the men all wind up in one room and the women in another?" Catherine took a sip of her tea.

Nora always thought that there was probably an unlabeled gene that had men gravitating to the room with the TV and women to the room with the food.

"I suppose we could all grab a beer and join the men on the back porch." Aunt Eileen waved an arm in the direction of the extra fridge.

"No thanks." Becky shook her head. "I prefer a comfy chair, a warm beverage, and something sweet."

"Besides your husband?" Catherine teased.

Becky rolled her eyes and dipped her head, but not fast enough to hide the blush that rose on her cheeks.

"My suspicion is tonight they're talking about the case that's haunting DJ." Aunt Eileen grabbed one of the cookies from the top of the dish.

"I've never seen him this bothered. Not since Jake Thomas." Becky curled her feet under her. "This is really getting under his skin."

Nora reached for her mug. "I've lived in this town long enough to know that most of the men live by a code of honor when it comes to the women and the Farradays seem to take it up one notch."

"True." Aunt Eileen nodded. "So what are we going to do about it?"

"We?" several voices echoed.

"We," Aunt Eileen repeated. "The police need decoys or stingers or whatever you call an officer on a stakeout and last time I looked, we're all women."

"Last time I looked," Catherine set her drink down, "none of us are police trained."

Joanna ran her fingers along the arm of the sofa. "She does have a point."

"That we're women?" Becky said.

"That there are a lot of us. You know, safety in numbers."

Aunt Eileen sat back, a satisfied expression on her face. "Now if we all put our heads together…"

The older woman's words were left hanging. Nora recognized the look on Aunt Eileen's face. Through the years she'd seen that determination at least a hundred times before. Somehow, she had the distinct feeling that the force of Eileen was about to strike, and that Nora and the others were going to get sucked in like a whirlpool. For the first time since this whole messy business started, she almost felt a little sorry for the bad guys.

CHAPTER SIXTEEN

"I have an overwhelming urge to synchronize our watches." But doing that would make this seem like a game, and Nora was fully aware there was nothing entertaining about the task they were going to undertake.

Using the rearview mirror, Becky added another coat of lipstick. The repetitive gesture the only thing that hinted she might be as nervous as Nora. "And I keep hearing the theme from *Mission Impossible* playing in my head."

"Oh great." Grace finger-combed her blonde hair. "Now I'm going to hear this stilted voice repeating in my head, *should you or any of your team be caught or killed, the Secretary will disavow any knowledge of your actions*."

"Actually," Meg grinned nervously, "it's any of your IM force."

Toni shook her head. "I prefer team. IM force makes it too easy to think of this mission as impossible."

"It's really quite simple." Catherine sounded much more convincing than her shaky smile implied. "There's safety in numbers. We have every type of girl represented."

"It's been a heck of a long time since I've been called a girl," Aunt Eileen teased.

Frank shot the Farraday matriarch a stern glare. "I want to say one last time for the record, this is an insane idea and you really should let DJ and the authorities handle this."

Like a well choreographed routine, every woman's head shifted to the left then right in an adamant rejection of Frank's plea.

"It's still not too late to at least call in more backup," he repeated for the umpteenth time since they'd left Tuckers Bluff.

Once again, same routine, same heads shifted left then right and back again.

"You know as well as we do," Aunt Eileen looked pointedly at Frank, "if we told anybody else our plan, our husbands would lock us in the house and throw away the key."

Frank sighed. "Smarter men than me."

"Too late now to change your mind." Aunt Eileen shrugged. As soon as all the Farraday grands were down for the night, the ladies had met up with Frank and been on their merry way.

"I'm not changing anything. Though I may regret not telling DJ what y'all are up to, there is no way I would let you do this without at least some back up."

Bless his Marine training. Nora felt a little better about this scheme knowing that someone on their team excelled, or at one time excelled, in hand to hand combat.

"Are we ready?" Aunt Eileen slapped her hands together and grinned broadly. "If that SOB is here, let's nail his astorbar to the wall."

All heads nodded. Oddly enough, the bit of jitters Nora had felt on the ride to Butler Springs were completely gone. They could do this. "Let's rock and roll."

Aunt Eileen and Frank were the first out of the car. The plan was for them to get a table that allowed a clear view of all the women. After five minutes, Meg entered, then Becky and so on until she and Grace walked in together so no one would be left alone in the parking lot, but split up as soon as they were inside.

This entire effort really did feel like an episode of *Mission Impossible*. She wouldn't be at all surprised if the theme song starting playing overhead instead of the club's popular country music. Already couples were two stepping their way around the dance floor. She opted for a seat at the bar instead of a table. From where she sat she could see Aunt Eileen and Frank right away. It took a few moments to locate the others. Everyone had their cell phones nearby and a group text already started. Periodic check-ins were mandatory even though they had eyes on each other. It would only take a minute of inattention for things to go south quickly.

"What are you having tonight?" The bartender's voice caught her off guard. She'd been concentrating so hard on keeping an eye on everyone that she'd forgotten her role in all of this.

"Club soda with a twist." Tonight was not the time for a wine.

"Here you go. Do you want me to start a tab?"

For a club soda? "Sure." She handed over her credit card and returned her attention to the tables. Only Meg was gone. Right away she glanced at her phone. No texts yet. They'd only been in the place all of maybe fifteen minutes. Meg couldn't possibly have needed to use the ladies room already, and even if she had, the rules of engagement were clear – no one leaves the main room alone. That's what the phones were for. Searching out Aunt Eileen, Nora followed the direction of the older woman's gaze. She was zeroed in on Meg and a tall man with dark hair who looked to be about a decade older than Meg. Oddly enough it hadn't occurred to Nora that their target could be a well-dressed mature man. For some insane reason she had visions of testosterone overloaded frat boys with a sense of entitlement. Suddenly the whole effort took on a new spin. They had to catch this guy tonight. They just had to.

She kept her eyes on Meg and the man through one dance, then two, and then noticed Becky had also moved onto the floor. Daring to pull her gaze away she searched out the other women. Grace had a cowboy, hat and all, at her table. Only someone who had known Grace since they were kids would recognize the plastic, how-long-do-I-have-to-be-nice-to-you smile on her face. Splitting her attention three ways wasn't as easy as she'd expected it. Especially when she took into consideration that three men were engaging the bait, but two more not counting her were bait too.

A sigh of relief escaped her lips when she spotted Meg returning to her table alone. Part of her wanted to catch this guy more than anything else, but another part of her wanted tonight to be uneventful and for everyone to go home unscathed. Of course, the best case scenario was to catch the creep and everyone, except the bad guy, go home unscathed.

"How ya holding up?" Surprise at hearing Frank's voice almost knocked her out of her seat.

"Fine."

"You look as nervous as a cat in a room full of rockers. You sure?"

"Just worried about everyone, I guess."

Frank waved a finger at the bartender. "Cola no ice and whatever you have on draft." The guy nodded and Frank turned his back to the bar, scanning the surroundings. "Service around here is awful. Waitress walked right past our table three times and didn't even glance our way."

"Maybe you don't look like a big tipper?" she teased.

"I have a feeling it's going to be a long night." Frank's eyes opened wide. "What the heck."

Following the direction of his gaze, Nora realized someone was trying to hit on Aunt Eileen.

"So help me, if I don't get that woman home in the same condition she got here in, Sean Farraday will make facing the Taliban seem like a walk in the park."

Nora couldn't help but laugh. She was pretty sure the cowboy at her side was harmless, but she was even more sure that Aunt Eileen could hold her own. Sure enough, another moment and the cowboy tipped his head and turned on his heel. She was pretty sure she heard Frank relax, even though his eagle eye stare told her he was not going to relax until they were all home.

"Don't you look like death warmed up." Abbie slid a cup of coffee in front of Neil. "Or do you need something stronger?"

"Long day." The day had started before sun up at the ranch, then moved on to a day of filming, and then he'd spent most of the evening in the office upstairs watching the dark apartment across the street. He knew that several of the women in town got together for Friday ladies night, and that Nora was perfectly safe and should be home soon, but still, he would simply feel less restless once she was home tucked in for the night. "Better give me a slice of pie to go with that."

"Have you had dinner?"

"Depends."

"On what?"

"Does a candy bar count?"

Abbie laughed hard. "No. I'll bring you a piping hot bowl of Shannon's beef stew. That should hit the spot."

"Shannon? The Shannon who usually waits tables?"

"Frank took the night off."

"Does he *do* that?" Neil hadn't lived here all his life but he had been here long enough to know that some things were a simple fact of life—death, taxes, and Frank in the kitchen at the café.

"Not usually. But he said he had some personal business to take care of today. He left the kitchen pretty well stocked for the night and Shannon is pretty good about filling in when we're short-handed. This is the first time she's behind the grill."

He supposed stranger things than Frank taking a night off happened. Nothing hit the spot quite like piping hot coffee. Cradling the mug in his hands, a burst of laughter from the other end of the café caught his attention. The ladies afternoon social club were playing cards. Without his aunt. From what he understood of the group, card playing was a daytime activity and his aunt never missed a game.

Abbie set silverware and a bowl of stew in front of him.

"Thanks." He nodded and tipped his head in the direction of the ladies. "Apparently tonight is a night for all kinds of firsts."

Her gaze lifted to the cackling women. "Yeah. Maybe there's a full moon or something."

"Or two." He laughed. "They do seem to be having a lot more fun than usual."

"I think the card game was just an excuse to get out on a Friday night. They've barely played any hands."

Sally May waved her arm in the air.

"Speaking of which," Abbie tapped the counter with her hand, "I'd better see what the merry maids of Tuckers Bluff want."

The bell over the door dinged and Neil looked up. He chuckled to himself. That old fashioned bell had folks conditioned like Pavlov's dog. It rang and just about every head in the place paused their meals and conversation to see who was joining them.

At the door, DJ spotted him and giving a casual glance to the ladies on the other side of the café, headed in Neil's direction. "Late dinner?"

"Abbie's doing. I was happy with a candy bar. You?"

"Marriage is a funny thing." DJ sat on the stool beside him.

Neil raised one brow at his cousin.

"You get used to certain things. Like knowing your wife is in the house even if she's not in the same room. Eating dinner with her smiling face across from you. Her fussing because tonight was your night to cook and you put too much kick in the taco soup."

Neil nodded. As a bachelor he couldn't relate to the wife part, but he certainly understood the concept of getting used to the ordinary things in life with one particular person.

"I know I got along just fine before Becky, but danged if I remember how."

How indeed. Neil could almost ask himself the same question. How had he enjoyed life before Nora?

"So, with Caitlin and her cousins spending the night at the ranch, here I am, escaping an empty house while waiting for my wife to come home so I can crawl into bed and get some much wanted sleep."

The bell dinged again and low and behold, another Farraday. Adam spotted the two of them and strolled over.

"You too?" DJ laughed.

Adam nodded. "House is too quiet. We don't even have

any guests to make noise."

"I gather Fiona is at the ranch tonight as well?"

"Yep. They're learning early to do sleepovers at Grandma and Grandpa's."

"Great bonding for the kids." DJ smiled. "I just hope Dad knows what he got himself into. Even if Aunt Eileen did wait till after bedtime to head out for girls' night."

"How late do they usually stay out?"

DJ shrugged. "Depends on whose house they're at."

"Or," Adam chuckled, "how much wine they've had."

Abbie walked over, a near empty coffee pot in her hand and a deep frown on her face. "Did any of you know girls' night was at the Boot N Scoots?"

All three heads shook from side to side. DJ's eyes narrowed.

Abbie blew out a low sigh. "I was afraid of that."

"Are you sure?" The muscles in DJ's jaw twitched under pressure. "It was agreed everyone would be staying away from there for now."

"I'm afraid I am. The ladies chatting away at the table seemed to think I knew since Frank asked for the night off."

"Knew what?" Neil didn't like the look on Abbie's face or the way the hairs on the back of his neck were standing on edge.

"They clammed up when I asked for clarification, but I think they've concocted a plan to catch the guy drugging women and Frank is their back up."

"Holy…." DJ shot up from the seat and strode intently across the café. Adam and Neil followed close behind.

"You should have kept your mouth quiet." Ruth Ann glared at Sally May.

"How was I supposed to know that no one had sworn Abbie to secrecy?"

Ruth Ann blew out a long sigh and shook her head.

"Ladies, I need to know what exactly is going on."

Dorothy leveled her gaze with DJ. "I don't suppose you'd believe nothing much?"

His expression stern, the police chief shook his head.

"I didn't think so." Dorothy shrugged. "In a nutshell,

we all decided that Butler Springs police are never going to catch this guy and meanwhile young women are being hurt."

DJ didn't say a word but Neil could see the man was biting down hard on his back teeth and probably his tongue.

"The plan is to split up and wait for this creep to hit on one of them and then the police will have their evidence and he can be locked up where he belongs."

Neil didn't know whose eyes grew wider but he was pretty sure all three of their jaws came closing to hitting the floor.

"What?" DJ said less than calmly.

"Now don't get your holster in a twist." Sally May pointed at DJ. "We're in on the group texts. They're checking in with each other every fifteen minutes and if anything goes wrong, we'll know to tell you."

"And what in the name of all that is holy am I supposed to do from here?" Shaking his head and muttering something Neil couldn't quite make out, DJ spun around, putting his phone to his ear and started walking. "Steve. It's DJ. We have a situation."

Neil and Adam followed him out the door as he explained what he knew to the Butler Springs police chief. On the curb, DJ hung up and looked to the two men. "They're having a full moon kind of night. Half his force is chasing down drag racers in three different parts of town. He'll do his best to get someone to the Boot, but there's not a whole lot of priority for six crazy women playing undercover."

"Whose car are we taking?" Neil asked. There was no need to ask if they were going or who was going. That was a no brainer.

"Mine. I have sirens."

Neil hadn't quite closed the backseat door when the car took off. No matter how fast DJ drove, it wouldn't be fast enough.

CHAPTER SEVENTEEN

"This is not going the way I had hoped." Meg ran her fingers through her hair and reapplied her lipstick.

"I know what you mean." For over an hour Nora and the Farraday women had made nice with more men—within reason—than any of them had probably intended. Not a single one had gotten anywhere near friendly enough to spike their drinks. And from what they could see, neither had anyone else. Early on they'd made it a point to not only watch out for each other, but to keep an eye out for anything suspicious with the other women in the place too.

Meg slipped her lipstick into her purse. "No wonder the cops are having a hard time finding this guy. I hadn't considered the possibility that he may not be here at all."

"All we can do is play the odds. DJ said that the most common connection with the victims was the Boot and always on a Friday night. So here we are." Nora did wish this guy would do something. She, like everyone else, wanted this character behind bars.

"We'd better get back inside before Aunt Eileen comes looking for us."

On their way back to their seats, Meg and Nora stopped at the table where Aunt Eileen and Frank sat overlooking the place.

"How long do you think we should stick it out?" Meg asked her in-law.

Aunt Eileen shook her head. "I don't know, but," her chin lifted to a man across the room by the bar, "what do you think of that guy?"

"I need more details," Nora said. "There are a lot of

guys in that general direction."

"The good looking one. Really good looking one." Aunt Eileen reached for her club soda. "Pressed jeans, no hat, blue shirt, toothpaste commercial smile."

"Third from the end of the bar?" Nora asked.

Aunt Eileen nodded. "Doesn't he look a little too perfect to be standing on his own not talking to any woman?"

"Since when is being good looking a crime?" Frank asked.

"I've been watching him for almost twenty minutes. He's not talking to anyone, he's nursed that same drink, and it just doesn't feel right."

Nora glanced at the guy. Now that Eileen had pointed him out, he did seem to stand out a bit. Then again, how easy was it for guys to ask total strangers to dance or for a drink? "Should I go make nice?"

"No," Aunt Eileen and Frank echoed quickly.

Aunt Eileen turned her attention to the others still scattered about. "If he is our man, he has to make a move on his own."

"Then we'd better get back to our spots." Nora nodded at her card playing friend and hurried back to the bar. Only now she was watching the guy at the end. Eileen was right about one thing, he looked awfully pretty to be standing there all alone.

About a half an hour later, Catherine and Becky went to the ladies room and the stranger was still nursing his drink and watching the crowd. Nora couldn't help but wonder if Aunt Eileen was right and this guy was more than just a bachelor out for a little two stepping.

Another half hour and it was Grace and Toni's turn in the restroom. So far Nora had danced with three different guys, and even let one of them buy her a drink. They'd talked a few minutes and then to her surprise, he excused himself and hit on some other woman at the other end of the bar. Even in a pick up joint she couldn't get a man's real attention.

"Ready for another?" The bartender paused in front of her.

She hadn't realized she'd finished her drink. "Yes, please."

"Club soda with a twist." For the first time all night he smiled at her.

What the heck, she smiled back and made a note to leave the guy a nice tip. So intent on watching her friends, she hadn't noticed the crowd had begun to thin out. No wonder the bartender had the time to serve her without her flagging him down. Turning her attention back to the general public, Mr. Too-Good-Looking gestured to the bartender, pulled a bill from his wallet and set it out in front of the server, nodded and walked away.

So much for Aunt Eileen's instincts. It actually surprised Nora. For as long as she'd known her, that woman had a keen intuition. So much so that at times Nora felt like the lady had a crystal ball in her pocket.

Glancing down at her phone, she read the screen. *Things are winding down. Looks like our plan's a bust. PS We've been ratted out. DJ and Adam and Neil are on their way.*

Oops. That wasn't how things were supposed to play out. She took a single long sip of her drink and settled in to wait for the men. Things would have been much easier to explain to the guys if their plan had been successful. Feeling like the stakes weren't quite so high anymore, she stole a minute to exit the group screen and scroll up to check for other messages. She'd missed a couple of texts from Neil. The first one asked *Are you all right*? The second message read. *We're on our way*. Third one buzzed as she held the phone in her hand. *Nora*?? Knowing the Farradays like she did, all the guys were probably freaking out in a tall, dark, and silent way.

Not wanting Neil and the others to burst a blood vessel, she started to tap a response. *I'm fine. We,* her finger slipped, *all are*. She went to put the phone down on the bar and wave the bartender over to ask for the bill, but the phone fell out of her hand and landed with a thud.

The bartender's head snapped around and he inched closer to her. "Everything okay, miss?"

Her mind thought *I don't know*, but the words wouldn't form. Instead she nodded. Slowly. Like a cold shower it suddenly struck her, she most definitely was not okay.

Eileen sent the last text for the night. *Time to go home.*

"I can't lie. I'm glad nothing happened." Frank took a long last sip of his drink. "For one thing, it doesn't seem right to spend all night in a public house and only nurse one beer."

"Public house?" Eileen chuckled. "Since when have you taken on a bit of the Brit?"

"Since your nephew opened the one and only public house in West Texas." He smiled and tipped his empty glass at her, then frowned.

Eileen followed his gaze.

"I can't believe it didn't work." Grace sank into an empty chair.

Striding up beside her sister-in-law, Becky shook her head. "You and me both."

All the women were either pulling up a chair or making their way to Eileen's table. Except Nora. Frank continued frowning. "Why isn't she moving?"

"That's what I'm thinking." Eileen tapped a new text. *You okay?*

Nora didn't move. Didn't react. Didn't reach for the phone.

"I don't like it," Eileen spoke softly, her back teeth biting down hard. They'd planned for this, hoped for this, but now that it might be happening, she felt an unexpected rage wrapped in a thick blanket of concern. Now was not the time to lose her cool.

Still frowning at Nora, Frank shook his head. "She wasn't talking to anyone."

"That guy." Eileen tore her gaze away to search out the character who'd bought Nora a drink then went off to hit on some other woman. It took a long moment, but Eileen spotted him cozying up to a blonde in the back booth. If he'd slipped something into Nora's drink it would be a surprise to Eileen. Who were they looking for? Could something else be wrong with Nora? Eileen shifted to the edge of her seat. Another minute and she was marching up there and finding out for herself what the hell was happening.

The seconds ticked by slower than a gimp snail. All eyes were glued on Nora, still on her stool, and then, she teetered slightly. If she wasn't drugged, what was she up to?

The bartender leaned over and said something to her.

"Looks like the bartender's noticed something is off." Like everyone else at the table, Frank wasn't taking his eyes off of Nora.

Meg sighed. "With the bartender helping her, if someone else did this to her, he's probably spooked. We won't have the proof for the cops. We'll never figure out who doped her."

"If," maintaining her litigator calm, Grace pointed a finger at her sister-in-law, "I repeat, *if* someone actually doped her. She might have another reason for not joining us."

"Like a lead?" Becky looked hopeful.

Meg shook her head. "Doesn't compute. Why wouldn't she text us what's going on?"

"I don't know." Grace remained focused on Nora. "Doesn't make sense to me either, but remember the plan. We watch her like a hawk, follow her like her shadow, and as soon as we have proof someone is up to no good—that will hold up in a court of law—we swoop in. Key thing is no matter what, don't let her out of our sight."

Eileen pushed away from the table and still keeping an eye on the bar across the dance floor, grabbed her purse. "Time to find out."

"Wait." Frank's beefy arm shot out and stopped Eileen from moving forward.

"What do you mean, wait?" Her gaze went from his arm stretched out in front of her, back to the movement at the bar. "Hmm. Get your things, ladies."

The bartender had come around to where Nora sat and sliding an arm around her waist, helped her off the stool.

"Everyone stays in pairs." Eileen kept her gaze forward. "And like Grace said, no one takes your eyes off those two. Let's boogie."

Practically holding her breath and praying she hadn't gotten them into something that would not end well, the Farraday women maneuvered through the crowds, following the bartender and Nora.

The bartender looked over his shoulder and Eileen froze. "Until we know what's going on, don't get too close."

With the evening winding down, the bouncers were no longer guarding the entry. The bartender and Nora walked out the door without anyone noticing.

"Maybe he's helping her get a cab." Frank didn't look nearly as optimistic as his words.

Out the door, they paused, not wanting to get too close, but wanting to see what were the man's intentions. Eileen held her cell phone to her ear and pretended to be talking. The bartender, oblivious to the women dispersed around the front entry way, stopped at the curb's edge.

"What's he waiting for?" Meg almost whispered.

"Maybe Frank's right. A cab?" Becky stepped out of the walk way and pretended to be looking for something in her handbag.

"Oh, crap." Eileen shifted in place. "Look who's over there."

"Over there where?" Grace peeked over her aunt's shoulder.

"The far corner of the building. Standing in the shadows."

"Mr. Too Good Looking," Grace muttered. "They could be a team."

"Isn't one pervert bad enough," Catherine practically growled. "A team of two is even more sickening."

"Either way," like all of them, Grace kept her eyes ahead, "none of this is looking good."

"He's moving." Aunt Eileen waved the women on.

Grace squinted into the dark parking lot. "Where the hell is he taking her?"

"Practically dragging her is more like it." Frank's tone dripped with annoyance.

Aunt Eileen sped up her stride. "Pick up the pace. We can't lose them."

"We should break this up a bit. I mean," Becky hurried to keep up, "won't it look a little suspicious if he turns around and sees seven people following him?"

Catherine shook her head. "There is no way under the sun this guy is going to suspect a bunch of women walking together of plotting against him."

Frank cleared his throat. Loudly.

"Sorry." Catherine shrugged at him. "And a man."

"He's headed for that motel."

"Crap." Catherine huffed. "That must be the strange place the victims have been waking up in that DJ mentioned."

"We've got him!" Eileen could hear the satisfaction in her voice. They were going to nail this SOB.

"Would now be the time to call in the police?" Becky asked.

Eileen shook her head. "Nope. We've discussed this before. How close is too close and how close isn't close enough. Like Grace said earlier, no cops until the guy can't explain his way out of it."

"Has to hold up in a court of law." Grace repeated. "Right now, no matter how bad or obvious it looks to us, he can claim he was just helping her to her car or waiting for a cab or a friend. We have to wait a bit longer."

"I don't know." Frank shook his head. "He's clearly not walking her to her car or calling her a cab and a blood test is going to show she's got something in her system besides soda water with a twist. I'm all for beating the truth out of the asshat."

Even though Eileen agreed there'd be a great deal of satisfaction watching the creep get the treatment he deserved, she preferred the idea of him rotting in jail for a very long time. "We have to at least wait until we see exactly where he's taking her."

The guy paused, and all seven of them spun around, turning their backs to him, pretending to be doing anything other than following him, including Catherine spilling out her purse on the ground.

On the ground helping Catherine gather up the belongings, Eileen kept her eyes on the bartender and Nora. "He's got a keycard to unlock the door. This isn't spur of the moment if he already has a key." She didn't need to see anything more. Going inside had to be enough for the police, and if it wasn't she didn't care anymore. They'd found the creep, the cops could figure the rest out on their own. "Let's move. Now."

Bolting across the last little bit of the narrow parking lot, Eileen maneuvered between two parked cars, her nieces on her heels, Frank at her side. "As soon as he closes the door, I'll knock. Say I'm room service."

"This place doesn't have room service." Frank shook his head.

"That's not the point. I need to get him to open the door before he has time to do anything and I can't just shoot it open." She stared as their target fidgeted with the door, thanking God that dealing with Nora's almost dead weight was slowing him down. "I'll say it's pizza. Everyone orders pizza in a place like this." The door swung open. They had a couple of minutes at best to get inside and call the cops. Eileen waved to either side of the door. "Y'all spread out on either side of me. Becky, keep your finger ready to hit 911. Once he opens it wide, we all rush in."

"Got it." Several heads bobbed.

"I should knock." Frank held a hand out to Eileen. "I'm hopefully more intimidating."

"No. He might not open the door for a man."

"Fine." She could see by the tight press of his lips his agreement came with a heavy dose of reluctance. "Just hurry up."

"And what the hell are you people doing?"

Eileen's head whipped about. Damn it. They didn't have time for this.

Mr. Too Good Looking stood behind her. Fortunately, Eileen didn't need to say a word. Frank had the guy in a headlock, his hand over Good-Looking's mouth and Frank nodded at her. "Go on, we're out of time."

The guy squirmed and groaned out a complaint. Frank tightened his grip. "Unless you want me to snap you in two like a chicken bone, shut up."

"Ready?" Eileen looked left and right. Everyone nodding, she knocked.

A small part of Nora's mind knew she was in trouble, but most of her brain was challenged putting the pieces together. Everything was so confusing. Any moment she expected to float to the ceiling and watch the world below. Everything was so heavy. She could hardly keep her eyes open. On top of that she must have sat down funny, her legs were numb. But so were her arms, and something was banging in her head.

Someone was in the room with her. She couldn't quite make out much more than a tall blob. And that incessant banging. What was it?

She shook her head trying to clear the fog. More banging, only it wasn't in her head. It was the door. Someone was at the door. What door? She sucked in a deep breath, air, she needed air. Had to clear her head.

"Pizza," she heard someone say pizza. Good, she was hungry. At least, she thought she was hungry. A muffled sound like the teachers on a Peanuts special was followed by another voice. More clear. Maybe. Something about free. She liked free.

Sit up. She needed to sit up. That would help. Her legs still felt so heavy, but she managed to swing them over the side of the bed. She was on a bed. Taking in another deep breath, she could make out the tall blob opening a door. The pizza—she was hungry, wasn't she? Yes. Her head was clearing. She was definitely hungry. Sitting up and hungry, and who the hell was at the door? A man? What man?

The door opened wide and a stampede of people rushed in.

"Don't move!" someone shouted.

A loud thud ricocheted from somewhere in the room. To her right. A pile of laundry on the floor. Not laundry. Laundry didn't move. Did it?

"Where's the rope?"

Rope?

"Here you go." Another, prettier person handed something off to the pile of laundry and then held something to her ear. "I'd like to report a kidnapping."

"Any new texts?" DJ asked for the tenth time in as many minutes.

Neil shook his head the same as he had the previous nine times. "Nothing since they texted they were ready to leave and then followed it immediately with 'stand by'."

"It's that 'stand by' that is making me nervous." DJ's grip on the wheel tightened. "When I get everyone home I may lock them up just to keep them safe from themselves."

"I'll throw the key away for you." Adam hadn't said much until now. The worry painted on his face mirrored the emotions Neil battled. He knew his aunt was one tough woman, but he hadn't thought her crazy. And he certainly hadn't expected her to put anyone she cared about in danger.

Lights flashing since they'd hit the city limits, DJ turned the corner only to be greeted by a bigger show of flashing blue and red lights lining the motel parking lot. Police cars were stopped at awkward angles along with the heart stopping sight of an ambulance. "Oh Lord."

Adam banged his hand on the dashboard. "We're too late."

Tires screeched as DJ slammed on his brakes. Not waiting for the car to fully stop, Neil threw the door open and shot out of the car. DJ and Adam on his heels, the three of them galloped over to the mass of people and officers huddled around the motel room door. As he'd done the entire car ride, he bargained with God once again.

"Well, how the hell was I supposed to know you were a policeman." Frank bellowed off to the right. "You people are supposed to announce yourselves."

"You didn't give me a chance!" a tall man dressed for a night out shouted back.

On his left, Becky ran out of the room and threw herself into DJ's arms. That was a good sign, Neil told himself. Two officers held their hands up, palms out, and DJ held his badge up for the officer to see. "They're with me."

"Don't know what you needed me for." Shaking his head, and almost smiling, a tall man in uniform walked out of the room and over to DJ. "When you called me to check up on your wife and aunt, the last thing I expected to find was our perp hog tied on the floor and four women pointing guns at him. *Four*," he repeated more intensely. "And then we have this jarhead sitting on my tied up police detective."

"Watch it," Frank snarled.

"I could throw the book at all of them. Interfering with a police investigation, assaulting an officer, thank God they didn't shoot anyone or we'd have discharging a weapon. And of course, there's breaking and entering."

"That's not true, Chief, and you know it," Aunt Eileen called from inside the room. "The SOB opened the door willingly."

"Yes, ma'am." The reproved man shook his head at DJ, who didn't look any happier than his police chief friend.

Meg had found her way into Adam's arms. "Did you bring Brooks?"

Those four little words made Neil's heart skip a beat. Who needed a doctor?

CHAPTER EIGHTEEN

Never had Nora's eyelids felt so heavy.

"Hi there." The decidedly male voice made her smile.

"Hi." Blinking hard, she looked at the ceiling for a few long seconds before turning her head to see Neil, holding her hand, on the edge of his seat, and concern oozing from every pore. She blinked again and glanced around her. It took a few minutes to realize she was not in her room or any other room she recognized. A hint of panic gurgled deep in the pit of her stomach as her mind scrambled to make sense of where she was and what had happened. "Where are we?"

"Guest room at the ranch. Do you remember anything?"

Nora thought hard. "We went to Butler Springs."

"That's right." Neil smiled. "We've been waiting for you to wake up."

"What time is it?"

"Six."

"That's too early. Why are you here?"

"Six pm. I've been here all night and day. You scared the hell out of me."

She struggled to remember. Not even small snippets of memory reared their faces. "I don't recall anything."

"Oh good." Aunt Eileen came in the door. "I thought I heard voices. How are you feeling?"

How *was* she feeling? She wiggled her fingers and toes. Other than feeling like she had a nasty head cold, all was well. "Not bad."

"Good, good. I'll go get you a nice bowl of chicken soup. Made it fresh this morning."

Aunt Eileen had barely crossed the threshold when

footsteps hurried into the room. Catherine came in first. "Boy did you have us all worried. I don't think Connor slept a wink last night."

"Same for Finn." Joanna followed her sister-in-law into the room. "The way he carried on, anyone would think I was one of the women who tried to bait a bad guy."

That was right. They went to the Boot N Scoots. "We were waiting for someone to hit on one of us."

Neil nodded. "What else do you remember?"

Several foggy pictures danced in her head, but nothing was coming into focus. "I don't remember anything. What happened?"

"You were drugged." Catherine sat on the other side of the bed. "Scared the heck out of us when we realized something was off and then the bartender helped you outside."

No matter how hard she tried, nothing was coming to mind.

"It seems our little mixologist was the one choosing women and spiking their drinks."

"You're looking pretty good." Becky came into the room, her husband following right behind her.

DJ moved to stand beside Neil. "Are you up to answering a few questions?"

She nodded. Not that her mind was likely to have any answers. Not the way she felt at the moment.

"Did the bartender say anything to you?"

She closed her eyes and thought really hard. "He was busy. Hardly said a word to me all night. Until…until…" The pictures slipped away. "I think he asked if I wanted another drink."

DJ nodded. "He must have waited till his shift was almost over to make a move. You had just enough Ketamine in your system to keep you off balance, but we're guessing by your actions and only sleeping half the day away that you must not have finished your drink."

Had she? Closing her eyes really tightly, she tried. She really tried.

Pressure tightened around her fingers and she realized

Neil was squeezing her hand. "If this is too much, you don't have to answer."

She shook her head. "I just can't remember."

"That's the drugs." DJ sighed. "The chief of police in Butler Springs was able to piece most of it together with the witness testimonies and a little gentle persuasion."

"Gentle persuasion?"

DJ chuckled. "When the bartender proved less than cooperative, the officer interrogating him threatened to let him go straight into the hands of Aunt Eileen and the rest of you." His laugh grew stronger. "You guys must have really done a number on him."

Now she wished she could remember. "What happened?"

"Well," Becky sat in the nearest chair, "it was amazing. First Frank and Aunt Eileen noticed you were acting funny. Then we spotted the bartender helping you outside. We weren't sure at first if he was helping or if he was our bad guy, but it didn't take long to figure out by the way he kept looking over his shoulder that something was up."

Neil's grip tightened, strangling her fingers.

With her other hand, she patted the top of his and wiggled the fingers he held onto so tightly. "Since I'm here, I'm going to venture a wild guess that everything turned out okay."

"Sorry." He smiled and eased his stranglehold.

"Anyway." Catherine picked up the story. Both she and Becky looked as excited as a kid recounting catching Santa by the chimney on Christmas morning. "We followed him to the motel across the alley from the Boot N Scoots."

DJ shook his head and Nora thought she saw his shoulders shudder. "His brother is the hotel manager. Gave him a pass key. He had access to any room he wanted, whenever he wanted, and there was no record of registering. That's why the police were having a hard time tracking him down. He only used a different motel if there were no rooms available. Again why he was hard to track."

"Anyhow," Catherine continued, "Aunt Eileen knocked and told him she had his pizza. At first we thought he wasn't going to buy it, but when she insisted it was paid for and he might as well get a free pizza, he opened the door."

Nora actually had the urge to giggle. She couldn't remember any of it, but she could just picture Aunt Eileen and the others storming the hotel room.

Becky waved a finger at Catherine. "You forgot to mention the detective."

"He wasn't a big deal. At first we thought he was the bad guy, but then he showed up as we were going in. Frank didn't know who he was so he slugged him."

Nora's mouth fell open, then snapped quickly shut.

"Yeah. The detective and Frank were going at it after everything was over. DJ talked the Butler Springs PD out of pressing charges."

Becky nodded. "On account of us helping catch the creep and all."

Right. Nora was still in shock the plan had worked.

"By the time the rest of the police arrived, Frank untied the detective, and Eileen and Grace had the creep hog tied."

"Was anyone hurt?" She could only imagine the fight the guy put up.

"Nah." Catherine shook her head. "He was good at math. Four guns, one Marine, and two pissed off women were unbeatable odds."

"Please don't remind me about the guns," DJ sighed.

"Why? We have licenses to carry."

"Need I remind you that four of you went into a public establishment carrying loaded weapons where guns are prohibited?"

Catherine winked at Nora. Apparently no one mentioned that she too had her firearm on her. That much Nora remembered. No one actually frisks the women who go into the dance hall and Aunt Eileen had professed this was one of those times when it was better to ask forgiveness than permission. They'd strode into the place with their concealed guns and right about now, she was glad they had. Things probably would have gotten a lot more messy if all of them hadn't brought a little—as DJ had just said—gentle persuasion.

"Are you sure you should be up and about?" Standing beside Nora at the foot of the stairs, Neil recognized his aunt was in full mother hen mode.

Brooks nodded. He'd come by with Toni to do a follow up on Nora. "I still don't want her alone tonight, but the drug will continue to wear off with no expected side affects except loss of memory."

"Will I ever remember what happened?" Nora's voice was low and soft and as far as Neil was concerned, he hoped she never remembered what she went through.

Brooks shrugged. "Nothing is set in stone, but it's unlikely."

From behind them, Aunt Eileen clapped her hands together loudly. "And now that everything is back to normal, let's eat."

"Oh good. I'm starved." Nora smiled and moved forward. She'd taken only one step when he reached out and snatched her hand.

"If you don't mind," he threaded his fingers with hers, "I'd like to stick close by for a bit."

Her gaze dropped to their clasped hands, then lifted to meet his, and her eyes twinkled with contentment. "I'd like that."

There were a lot of things he would like right about now. Not letting her out of his sight ever again was only one of them.

"Are you really hungry or just being polite?" He was prepared to whisk her away if going through the motions was too difficult.

"No," she smiled, "I really am famished. I haven't eaten in over twenty-four hours."

The conversation around the table shifted from the creep they'd nabbed the night before to how well Molly's recovery was coming along and how the folks from town had stepped up to help her keep the truck running while she recovered. The sisters and Aunt Eileen had done battle over who would care for Molly during her convalescence. In the end, neither won; the production company footed the bill for her to get professional care until she could return to running the truck. Though Neil had little doubt that all of the women would be keeping tabs on Molly regardless.

"I'd love to stay for dessert, but we have to get back to town before Helen's bedtime." Brooks kissed his aunt on the cheek.

"Next time," Aunt Eileen turned to Toni, "bring Helen."

"We will." Toni smiled. "This time it was just easier leaving her with Meg and Adam."

With everyone bidding their farewells and only the residents of the ranch remaining, Aunt Eileen came up to them in the living room. "Why don't you go on out to the back porch for some fresh air and I'll bring Nora the last slice of my blueberry sour cream pie. I saved it just for you."

"What about me?" Neil teased.

His aunt shook her head. "Apple pie or pound cake?"

"Nothing, thanks." He pulled Aunt Eileen into his arms for an old fashioned bear hug and whispered into her ear, "Thanks for taking care of her."

Aunt Eileen patted his arm. "She's a keeper. Even if you don't have Gray's blessing."

"That reminds me." Neil took a step back. "How often does Gray stowaway into town?"

"Stowaway?" Eileen's brows buckled in confusion.

"Yeah. My first night in town a few weeks ago, he was parked outside the pub like a statue."

"Oh." Nora turned to him. "That must have been the night of our first, uhm, dinner date. He was just staring at me when I pulled up to the curb."

A bright smile eased across Aunt Eileen's face. "Both of you saw him in town?"

They both nodded.

"Did anyone else see him?" Eileen asked.

What an odd question, he thought. "No, by the time Ryan and others left, Gray was gone."

Eileen's grin grew wider as she turned and walked away

mumbling something about, "Need to cook up some liver for those two tomorrow morning."

"I sure hope she's talking about the dogs. I hate liver." Nora sank onto the porch swing.

Neil slid into the empty space beside her. "You really did scare the heck out of us last night. All of you did. I don't think I've ever seen DJ drive so fast."

"That wasn't the plan."

"It was a crazy plan."

"But it worked."

"And what if it hadn't? What if they hadn't noticed him taking you? What if he'd actually…hurt you?"

"But he didn't. There's safety in numbers. And anyone worth their salt knows you don't mess with strong Texas women. We've got good pioneer genes."

"Still." He tried not to think about what could have happened and was thankful that everyone walked away in one piece and no one got hauled off to jail or worse. "Can we talk for a minute?"

"I thought we were." She smiled at him and his brain turned to mush.

It took a second to not get lost in that beautiful smile or the deep brown eyes that captured his attention that very first night. "I mean about us."

"Us?" Her smile slipped and he took a deep breath.

He nodded. "About this arrangement. The one where we have a few dates and then you dump me."

"Because I don't like the way you chew your food." She was teasing him again.

At least he thought her teasing mood was a good sign. "For me, nothing about the last few weeks has felt like pretending. If there's any chance you feel the same way, I'd like to give us a real try. Not a pretend try."

Her gaze locked with his, her smile slipped and her mouth dropped slightly open. "You do?"

"I do. I, uh," he swallowed hard, "I don't want to think about losing you."

"You don't?" A smile began to tip upward at one corner of her mouth.

He shook his head. “You see. I, uh, I’m well on my way to being totally boots over Stetson in love with you.”

Her mouth dropped open again and before he could kiss the surprise away, her mouth snapped shut and the rest of that smile took over. “I guess it’s a good thing I am too.”

“You are?”

She nodded. “Except I’m not well on my way. I’m already there.”

Torn between shouting Hallelujah or kissing her socks off, he opted for pulling her into his arms and lightly pressing his lips against hers, “I love you, Nora Brown.”

“Here you go—oops.” His aunt’s footsteps stopped short. “I’ll just leave this on the table here.”

Their foreheads touching, they both chuckled at Aunt Eileen’s reaction, then ignoring dessert delivery, their lips met again. In the distance his aunt could be heard happily repeating, “Twelve for twelve. Way to go, Gray.”

EPILOGUE

"Take a deep breath and chill." Owen waved a finger at his brother. "Any idiot knows this is going to work."

"Honey, I'm home," Nora's voice draped in a teasing giggle echoed through the nearly empty house. "Oh wow."

"See?" Owen slapped Neil on the back. "Let's show them around." From where he stood, Owen could see the wide eyed look on Nora's face. Neil had intentionally kept her and the rest of the family away once they'd started putting the house back together again. Especially this house where Neil had invested so much extra effort.

The big reveals were some of Owen's favorite moments. Seeing the sheer joy in the buyer's eyes could make even the grumpiest person smile. This time the Farraday brothers, or cousins as the show was called, had even more hanging on the line.

"Oh my." Aunt Eileen followed Nora into the house. "This is quite the change, isn't it?"

While the rest of the clan who'd made time to fit the big moment into their Saturday afternoon filtered inside, Nora sidled up beside Neil and grinned up at him. "I knew it would be gorgeous but it's still a shock to the system." Her eyes widened as her gaze darted to the kitchen backsplash. "You picked the blue."

All week Neil had been as antsy as a mouse in a maze. Any minute Owen had expected his brother to burst a blood vessel. With all the supply delays and production issues, completing the house had taken two weeks longer than originally projected. Keeping the blasted project on budget and avoiding any additional delay had pretty much tested

Owen's blood pressure on a daily basis, but the last few days had been hardest on Neil.

"You were right." Neil's eyes locked with Nora's. "The blue subway was the best choice."

Owen knew he should be showing the rest of the family around, but he was having a hard time dragging his attention away from his youngest brother. When Morgan, the oldest of the brothers, had fallen for Valerie, Owen had only been around sporadically. This time he'd had a ringside seat to the entire courtship and seeing his brother look at Nora with stars in his eyes and her gazing back with the same adoration had Owen teetering somewhere between yeehaw shouting joy and deep green envy.

"We went with the Carrara countertops." Neil's voice came out so soft and quiet as he shifted to point at the marble countertops that Owen could barely hear him and doubted any one else across the room even knew he'd spoken.

"These floors are gorgeous." Meg stared down at the floor and others oohed and aahed, pointing out the tone, the shade, the wood grain and just for the fun of it, a few of the kids started their best imitation of River Dance.

"Careful, sweetie," Aunt Eileen looked to the children, "we don't want to scratch the floors."

"No worries." Owen shook his head. "There's enough poly on this floor to last a century."

Meg smiled at him. "We'll let the new owners break in the floor."

Owen held back a chuckle. That was one way to maintain peace in a now crowded home.

"I want one of these." Becky stood in the hall, looking through a doorway. "Cedar closets are the best, and this one is huge."

Nora whipped around and peeked over Becky's shoulder into the walk-in space. "This is so cool for an old house."

"Good grief." Kelly called from another room. "Are all the closets walk in?"

Smiling from ear to ear, Neil nodded. "I have it on good

authority that big closets are lacking in this part of the county."

Nora had returned to her spot at his side and winked up at him.

"Real stairs!" Toni squealed. "I have never understood the Texan's fondness for pull down stairs. This is seriously cool."

Pulling Nora closer into his side, Neil kissed the top of her head and mumbled something Owen couldn't hear. Something that made her smile impossibly wider.

Everyone else was delighted walking through the old home, but Owen was taking in the couple still standing in the kitchen. Footsteps tapped overhead. In order to increase room and closet sizes, they'd opted to go ahead and turn at least a portion of the old attic into current living space. The decision seemed to be going over well as shoe heels clicked on the wooden treads and voices danced over each other as his relatives spilled into the hallway.

"Y'all have thought of everything. That tub in the master is to die for." Grace came up to Owen and waved Paxton over. "I can't decide if I want y'all to come in and update our house or just start new."

"You could get in on the ground floor of Three Corners. The developers are set to extend utilities and pave roads on Monday. Plans include space for a grocery store and other retail."

"You mean besides what's going in on Main Street in Sadieville?"

The two brothers nodded and Grace looked at Chase. "Wonder how bad the commute to the feed store would be."

Chase simply laughed, curled his wife into his side, and softly kissed her temple. "I'm sure it wouldn't be any worse than a commuter train ride into Manhattan."

Neil glanced up at his brothers and cousin. "Don't laugh too hard, Chase. There's talk of a Farraday section of town."

Grace's husband laughed from deep in his belly. "Works for me."

"What's this?" Nora had inched her way over to the

only decoration in the house. A simple black frame with hints of golden highlights held a tattered newspaper behind glass.

"That's a surprise." Neil stepped up behind her and pointed. "You'll want to read this."

Her lips barely moving, Nora muttered under her breath the words directly under Neil's finger. Owen knew the moment she'd come to the portion that had made Neil have the paper framed. Nora's jaw dropped and her eyes widened. "Euphemia May Callahan and Walter Ulysses Potter left on yesterday morning's stage after a private ceremony with…" She spun around. "Is this the chest?"

Neil nodded. "Apparently the young couple—she was only fifteen—eloped. The pastor married them minutes before the stage left so their parents couldn't stop them. They settled in California."

"Settled?" She went back to the frame and found another, less tattered portion of a clearly more recent paper. One many years later announcing the golden anniversary of Euphemia and Walter Potter of Sacramento, California. "How sweet is this?"

"Valerie tracked down their great-great-granddaughter. She thought it would be a fun extra bit for the show. The woman told her that the young couple had been neighbors and the parents had been feuding for years over who knows why. The reason the trunk was left behind was because they left with only the shirts on their backs and a little saved money. The great-granddaughter is coming to town to get the trunk. She's ecstatic to come see her family's roots."

By now folks had gathered around the brothers and the wall hanging, congratulating them on a job well done, and chatting away at how difficult it must have been for the lovebirds, which trickled over to how different teenagers were a hundred years ago. All agreeing that marrying young wasn't necessarily anything they wanted the world to revert to. The chattering suddenly slowed and Owen knew this was it.

Shifting to the other side of the room, he snagged a birds eye view of Nora's hands by her mouth, Neil on one knee, and his hand opening a small red velvet box. The guy had been so nervous the last few days, heaven knew he'd rehearsed what he wanted to say in front of the bathroom mirror only a hundred times or more. Owen just hoped after all the effort, his kid brother didn't blow it.

"They say when you find the right person, you'll know it. The first time I saw you across the pub at O'Fearadaigh's, I couldn't take my eyes off of you."

Abbie, who'd worked her way over to Owen's side for a better view, leaned into him and softly whispered, "He's not kidding. I was there."

"If you want to make this house a home, *our* home," Neil continued, "it's yours. If you want me to build you something better somewhere else, I will. If you'll agree to share my life with me, I promise to do everything in my power to make you happy for as long as I live."

Nora sucked in a deep breath, let her hand fall away from her face and leaned forward, arms waving in the air. A collective gasp filled the room as she stumbled over a small toy fire truck overlooked by one of the kids. Neil sprang from his feet just in time to catch her in his arms before she face-planted on the freshly polished floors. Taking in another breath, Nora looped her arms around Neil's neck and giggled. "I guess we'll have to change our vows to love, honor, and catch me." Her mouth met his, the room erupted in a cheer and Owen had to admit, he'd most definitely fallen off the fence into the envious side of the yard.

His phone buzzed and he glanced down at the text then slid the phone back into his pocket.

"You have that crossed look in your eyes again." Aunt Eileen replaced Abbie at his side. "Today is too happy a day to look so worried. Anything I can help with?"

He shook his head and forced his mind to focus on how happy his brother and future wife were, and his mouth immediately lifted into a sincere smile. His aunt was right about at least one thing: today was not the day to let reality bring him down. "No, ma'am. As you said, today is a happy day for the Farradays."

MEET CHRIS

Author of over thirty contemporary novels, including the award winning Aloha Series, Chris Keniston lives in suburban Dallas with her husband and two canine children. Though she loves her puppies equally, she admits being especially attached to her German Shepherd rescue. After all, even dogs deserve a happily ever after.

More on Chris and her books can be found at www.chriskeniston.com.

Follow Chris on facebook at ChrisKenistonAuthor.

Join Chris' newsletter! Enjoy inside peeks and photographs from Chris' world and stories. Some times she'll thank her subscribers with a free copy of a new 99 cent flirt.

For more on what she's up to from day to day, you can follow her Monday Blog at her website Chriskeniston.com or follow her on Facebook!

Please, if you enjoyed reading Neil, consider helping other readers find the Farraday Country series by taking a moment to leave a review. Reviews are a blessing to authors and readers alike. Even just a few words will do! Thank you.

CPSIA information can be obtained
at www.ICGtesting.com
Printed in the USA
LVHW111556270322
714530LV00005B/289